DEMONIC ANTHOLOGY VOLUME I
A Dark Humor Short Story Collection

DEMONIC
WILDLIFE
A FANTASTICAL FUNNY ADVENTURE

DEMONIC ANTHOLOGY VOLUME I
A Dark Humor Short Story Collection

DEMONIC WILDLIFE
A FANTASTICAL FUNNY ADVENTURE

Linda Hull	Richard Wentworth	Jeremy Rodden
Clint Doyle	Christina Bergling	Kim Plasket
Arielle Haughee	Teresa Edmond-Sargeant
J.P. Dildine	Maxine Grey	L.E. Perez	G.H. Finn

4 Horsemen
Publications, Inc.

Dedication

We dedicate this first Anthology under Battle Goddess Productions to the Authors and their families. Without you, our adventure would not be possible. We hope you share this book with pride and hope to see you in our future *Demonic Anthologies* as we grow!

Acknowledgments

No book or publication would be complete without a proper thank you to the volunteers, editors, and proofreaders who helped to create the finished piece. Thank you for your time, devotion, encouragement, and support to Battle Goddess Productions as well as our Authors found within.

Table of Contents

Readers Beware

Y ou are about to set foot on a bizarre adventure, a funny fantastical one filled with demonic animals. The first few stories are light, more about the giggles, but be warned. As you read further, the dark creepy side will sneak up on you...

The Spider Laughs

By Linda Hull

The spider who lives on my front porch laughs at me. No one hears it but me. No one else is supposed to. It has a deep, throaty, rumbling laugh similar to the way villains laugh just before they blow up orphanages or embezzle money from the elderly, only the spider laughs quieter. Real soft. No one hears it but me and I won't tell anyone because then the spider won't be the only one laughing at me.

The spider laughs at me because it knows. Oh yes, it is capable of awareness and it knows that I am afraid of it. I'm not afraid that it will bite me and kill me with its poison, because I know it is not venomous. Nor am I afraid that it will jump onto my face and suck all of the juice from my eyeballs leaving them to rattle in my head like shriveled, dried apricots, because I know this particular spider is not of the eyeball-sucking variety. (Those spiders live in your couch. Not my couch. Your couch.) I am just afraid that it will get on me. That is enough. The mere thought that a spider might get on me sends me into paroxysms of fear. I am absolutely convinced that if a spider ever does get on me I will go insane in that instant. The very moment of a spider's touch will transform me from a walking, talking, productive member of society to a quivering, slobbering mass of misfiring neurons that has to be intravenously fed. I know this to be true, deep down in the very core of my soul. The spider knows it too. That is why it laughs.

I have a Spider Dance. Everyone knows this Dance; though perhaps by a different name: The Lizard Dance, The Mouse Dance, The Bat Dance, and the increasingly popular Oh Crap, I Think That's A Killer Bee Dance. They are all the same – a frenzied, total blind panic, running frantically while slapping yourself Dance to get it OFF. I can be sent into my Spider Dance merely by spotting a web within my comfort zone (A twenty-foot invisible sphere emanating from my right ventricle.) Actually, touching a spider's web instantly neutralizes my nervous system and I pass out. As a child, I fell flat out of a tree because I touched a web. I felt it brush my arm and I simply let go of the branch supporting me. I fell nearly 10 feet down to the grass below. I woke up I-don't-know-how-many-minutes-later with my dog licking my face and flew straight into my Spider Dance, running across the yard slapping myself followed by my concerned and confused barking dog. You see, the Spider Dance can be delayed, but not prevented.

It is therefore, unfortunate that I live in Florida. Florida's soupy, steamy semi-tropical climate sanctions a simmering cauldron of pseudo-primordial stew and the entire state is consequently crawling with detestable organisms such as alligators and snakes and lizards and loud poisonous toads that sing all night long. There are trees that strangle one another, plants that eat bugs, and mite-infested Spanish moss dripping from every Oak. At the beaches, there are sharks and crabs and stinging jellyfish and who knows what is living in those clots of seaweed floating out there in the surf. And everywhere, I mean everywhere – sometimes even creeping out of the overflow drain when you are taking a bath, are roaches as big as my big toe that can, and do, FLY – usually right toward your face. I'm sure there is at least one in the room with you right now. But, what bothers me most are the spiders. Not tiny little dime-sized spiders found in normal parts of the world. I am talking about SPIDERS – industrial strength, chemical-resistant spiders with bodies the size of Vienna sausages, legs three inches long and web silk as strong as sewing thread. Sigourney Weaver would hesitate to approach one of these things. We locals call them Banana Spiders. Officially, they are labeled Golden Orb Spiders. They emigrated here in the '60s from Central and South America aboard cargo ships carrying exotic fruit, just as many of our human residents did. They are not poisonous (the spiders aren't, I make no such claims regarding the humans), or that is what the "experts" claim, anyway. I don't believe anyone could have ever voluntarily gotten close enough to one to really find out.

To cope with living in this jungle where something dreadful could jump, leap, drop, run, fly, swim, swing, or crawl out at you at any moment, I early on – right after the tree incident – developed a web detector sense for my protection. I can now spot a spider web from 73 feet away. I can even spot them in trees along the highway from a moving vehicle going 65 miles an hour. I constantly scan for them. It is not conscious; it is just another part of my life-support system like breathing and pumping blood, and changing the radio station every time Justin Timberlake comes on. I just do it. I see a web, my Spider Proximity Alert goes off and I instantly become watchful and wary. I also duck into a crouch. This has caused some repercussions in social situations that I will not discuss in this essay.

It's easy with web spiders. My SPA helps me locate them and at least they have the integrity to stay put. The evil, fat, hairy, brown sofa spiders are more insidious. You never know where they may come from. There is no shimmer of light glinting off of a drop of dew on a gossamer thread to give them away – they just appear. You can find them in the corner of your living room, under the couch, on the inside of your car's windshield, in your shoe, on the pillow next to your head – they could be anywhere. Even in your underwear drawer. They can get very close before you see them. They want it that way. It's easier for them to get on you. I don't like to think about those kinds of spiders.

There is a spider web in the corner of my front porch where I am sitting right now. The laughing spider is in it. It is a prime specimen of the Golden Orb variety and, with its legs spread out, it is exactly the size of my face. It knows I am writing about it. It wants me to come closer so it can read my notebook. I won't do it. I keep my left arm over the page so it can't see. It moves back and forth in its web trying for a better view. It is ten feet in the air on a wall twenty-one feet away from me. Just outside my Spider Proximity Limit. It has lived there for two weeks because spider insecticide only sprays fifteen feet. I watch it carefully when I enter and exit the house. I know it wants to get on me. I keep an eye on it in case it makes a sudden move. The spider laughs at me. It laughs because it knows.

Linda Hull

L inda Hull grew up in Miami, Florida, spending most of her time playing with imaginary friends and making up stories. Once in a while, she would write some of those stories down and distribute them among a very select, highly amused few.

Some of these amused few encouraged her to follow her dream of becoming a writer. So she went to Rollins College and got a BA in English/ Writing. Since then Linda Hull's work has been seen onstage at Universal Studios, Florida, the Orlando Fringe Festival and onscreen at a number of film festivals.

Balancing a full-time job with freelance editing, an attempt at a website, and writing something new, Linda is hoping to drag herself out of the starving artist category by offering her work at .99 on Amazon.com instead of free.

writenowlinda.wix.com
www.facebook.com/writenowlinda
www.amazon.com/Linda-Hull

Ninji

By Richard A. Wentworth

Derick's world had been dramatically changed in a blink of an eye. Okay, its happening wasn't that fast but when your unconscious and wake up to find yourself, safe! His small sailboat was tied off to a dock and he had no idea of when? How? Or why—He was alive.

Sure, he was sailing along, his small sailboat gliding through the beautiful crystal clear green water; with a full bright sun bringing on renewed heat and him feeling confident.

The storm came out of nowhere! One second the sea was flat, beautiful, and then it turned into a screaming banshee, trying to swamp him. The only thing that Derick found odd: was a strange buzzing shrill whistle sound, followed by an intense Humm of rapid beats which tossed his sailboat about, like a cork.

"The only thing, I do remember of how I reached this Island, not sure if it was divine intervention? Or luck? Or was it pure chance! Anyway, it all started when a freak storm, without any clouds, crossed my path. I was sailing smoothly along and all of a sudden the sea was turning sour; a strong wind developed, which forced me to clear sails, secure all hatches and ride out this phenomena of nature in my cabin." At this point in his narrative, Derick lets out a nervous laugh and sighs.

"My sailboat was my pride and joy—sure, some laughed at its small size, twenty-five feet, but to me it was a luxury yacht and my most valued possession. She was simple to operate and navigate: I installed a state-of-the-art GPS navigation system in case I could not figure out how to use a sextant."

Derick saw the sailboat, as an extension to his free spirit.

Many months ago, when he was visiting a marina, he found her. She had a special charm, taking his breath away and she was for sale. When he got permission to finally step on her deck: he felt at home; with his imagination running rampant. She was perfection; a sturdy hull, sharp lines and when he ran his fingers, curling them, gripping the helm—she purred and he was excited. Her colors—a soft walnut hue with streaks of golden sun rays, he fell in love with her.

A few months later with many weekend trips aboard her, to get to know her spirit, he felt they were ready to explore.

"This freak storm appeared quickly and was tossing me and my sailboat about like a cork on the vast sea. And with one violent shutting strike; with a force of a run-a-way-freight train, had caused me to be tossed about my tiny cabin. I now understand how a pin-ball feels like on a rollercoaster. I curled into a ball for protection. I must have hit my head, because when I came too, my head was sore and a trickle of blood on my forehead and I felt like a vice was squeezing my head, tightly. Anyway, as I began to feel like my old self; I noticed that the storm had passed and all the violent motions had vanished and the sea was at peace." Slowly, Derick was brushing a few stray strands of hair out of his eyes.

"With care: I sat there; going over what had transpired, appraising the situation, while listening for hurricane winds." A sigh escaped his tightly pressed lips and he inhaled deeply—one of those to clear the mind and organize his thoughts.

"Once I had calmed down; the next step was to check topside." Derick paused, shaking his head and his adventuress smile spreading.

"On weak legs, I popped the hatch, breathed in a healthy mind clearing deep breath of salty fragrant oxygen. My mind was reeling: by my calculations, before the storm struck. Land was over Six Hundred miles away: and there was no way, I was out for that long, nor drifted, or pushed that far." Derick stopped, shaking his head slowly.

"As I gathered in my surroundings, my sailboat was tied up—I check the lines and they were tight to an old wood dock. The lush Islands green vegetation inviting and ready to be explored. When I stepped onto the dock; I collapsed — my legs weak from inaction, adjusting from sea legs to land legs. I lay there, not sure for how long and I slowly stood, performing a Three-Hundred-Sixty-Degree turn, while taking in the splendor of the Island and yet something seemed amiss; then it hit me, the vegetation was immense. This turn of though reminded me of the Jurassic Park movies, a shiver of excitement ran threw me but I shrugged it off, due to over imagination. As I contemplated these thoughts, I returned to my sailboats cabin." Derick took one last look at the Island and disappeared into the sailboats cabin.

As Derick surveyed the scattered items, he began to replace them back into their cubby-holes, while scratching his head, trying to figure out what had happened.

As his mind was clearing, a thought occurred and he stepped over to where the compass was. The compass was slowly spinning. He gave it a faint tap, stopping it, for half a second, but it continued spinning, lazily. He sighed in frustration — he turned on the Global Positioning System. While he waited for the GPS to come on-line, a typical message flashed on the screen, 'Trying to reconfigure calculations. Sorry, system does not compute! Try again?' Derick sighed and ran his fingers through his hair. His exasperation was at a high level and...

"Get a grip, Derick! There has to be an explanation?" His eyes were looking for items to take with him; but his mind was saying "NO!" Finally, he spotted the yellow dive knife with an ankle strap; he picked it up and strapped it on. He nervously ran his fingers threw his hair, letting out a held deep breath, surveying the tiny cabin one more time and opened the cabins door.

"Ahh! You scared a few lives out of me!" Derick yelled, grasping at his chest, his heart racing. Yet — he felt a connection immediately that he could not explain.

One woman was standing in front of the door — ready to knock. Her smile was electrifying, intoxicating and real. She grabbed his hand, yanking him towards herself with surprising strength, then into a fierce bear hug. She was pressing, very intimately into him, and he was — offering no resistance.

His mind whirled; "It's a dream!" he responded absentmindedly, snuggling into her, liking this type of greeting.

"We must hurry, Ninji is coming!" she turned, pulling harder and more frantically. "Ninji is coming," she wailed.

Derick resisted the pulling, his mind uncomprehending. Her pulling growing more frantic with each passing second, repeating loudly, "Ninji is coming!"

Out of nowhere, her opened palm slapped his face, hard, bringing on stars and snapping him out of the dream. She was backing away, pointing out in the crisp, blue sky.

Derick followed her pointed arm, noticing a blur of color streaking towards them.

"What the Hell—is Ninji?" He asked suspiciously.

She slapped him again, harder than before and grabbed his hand, pulling...

"Quick! We must hide. Follow me!" Both leaped from the sailboat and charged down the dock, hand in hand, legs pumping, lungs straining, hearts beating wildly. Derick's adrenaline was controlling his wild running. And she set the pace, glancing over her shoulder every few steps, chanting, "Faster...! Faster...! We are almost there!"

The dock was a blur under their feet. Derick kept glancing back at his sailboat, which appeared safe for the moment and to the shape flying towards them. The flying colored thing was taking shape and closing on them. And the fear controlled their flight, making both move faster. In seconds, the sound had changed from running on a wooden dock, to one of running over hard sand, and then, a head long crash into a thick morass of jungle. The landscape swallowed them whole...

She led the way, Derick followed with samplings thrashing at his face, body and soul. They continued to penetrate at a fast clip, never slowing. She was ducking, weaving, holding a fast pace and holding his hand in a deadly vice grip. Minutes passed, then, she released her grip slightly and they came to a panting stop.

Derick was doubled over, sweat running free, his heart hammering, feeling excited. He glanced at the woman, she wasn't even fatigued.

"Ninji cannot follow us, we are safe! For now," she batted her eyes, took a deep breath and flung herself at him, her arms encircling around his neck, and... Both crashed to the ground. Derick was more surprised by her reaction, but hey, he wasn't going to complain. They lay face-to-face, her body warm, soft, inviting. Derick closed his eyes, ready to kiss her.

"Not now, later! Let's move! I know of a safer place." Her smile was growing when she said this.

Derick, slowly, lets her go and both stand quickly brushing the remnants of dirt from their clothing and she broke into a soft trot.

"I am Miko, by the way," and she raised her arms—spinning, as she leaped high in the air doing an easy Three Hundred Sixty Degree turn, landing softly and continued as if nothing had happened. Her smile was growing, eyes inviting, wild with promises of enchantment.

Derick groaned, his mind spinning, this woman, "Miko," was defiantly—breathtaking: long, flowing dark black hair, her skin a kissable brown and her eyes—hypnotic! Derick did not know where to start. Yes! Her eyes had a wild streak, brown in color with specks of gold. Derick knew when he finally got a chance to rest and look into them, he would be hopelessly lost, but at the time, he did not care. This thought made him stop suddenly, his mind spinning, *Siren, but they were on land, not the sea, so...*

She stopped, too, looking back, their eyes locking, "Trust me! I'll explain when we are safe."

Derick was looking about their impressive dwelling, a cave, as a matter of fact, but comfortable. Natural light filtered in, creating a romantic mood. The view outstanding, looking over the Island's interior. And if you went to the back of the cave, another view of the harbor came into view and his sailboat. However, the story she told him, sent shivers through out his body and mind. Suddenly, he felt like a tiny ant in a giant's world.

Derick stood, shaking his head, running his fingers through his hair, muttering, "A demonic Hummingbird? How the hell... and you want me to challenge it? But...it's the size of a bus!" Miko was nodding her head and had a beaming smile.

"Ninji was my pet and we guarded this Island. Until one day: a strange man appeared on the Island. Trapping Ninji and placing that charm around his neck and turned my once gentle Hummingbird into a demonic creature. Ninji was growing and growing, the island changing to fit Ninji's size. Of course, when Ninji had stopped growing; he attacked the man, carried him off, and, I assume, dropped the man, far off...in the ocean, after that... here we are. You are a long line of people Ninji has brought to the island; searching for that one person to break the spell, and he chose you!" As she finished her story, a single tear ran out of one eye.

Derick sat silently. He watched as her tear, ever so slowly, slid out, traveling down her cheek. Her emotions confused him, he wanted to hold her—to reach out, caress and... but... her story made him immobile and speechless and his face was drained of color,

Derick muttered, "Yea! Lucky for me!"

Miko could be heard—singing—her voice soothing.

As Derick listened to her song, a plan was forming as he surveyed the choice of weapons. None were calling out to him but when he stepped before a simple wooden staff, a bright beam of light erupted from it. He bent down, grasped the wood tightly. The staff felt light, strong, and right; he twirled it and he knew the choice was perfect. A picture reeled before his eyes and he was breathing…hard.

Miko had stopped singing and she walked up to him, glanced at him, smiled with an inviting temptation. She was nodding: pointing outside; he was gripping the staff tightly, breathing calmly.

Gathering his nerve, he stepped outside the cave. The island was quiet, no animals were heard and even the wind had stopped to listen. With determined steps, he took up a defensive position, legs spread—on the balls of his feet and commanded:

"Ninji, come to me…!" nothing happened—he lets out a deep tension draining breath, rolled his eyes and shoulders, thrusting out his chest and… commanded again, with force:

"Ninji come to me…"

Immediately, the Island began to rumble—unlike a true Earthquake, but a separation of air as Ninji advanced towards his prey. His oversized wings were splitting the air, creating sonic booms.

Derick stood his ground, he knew where the demonic Hummingbird would appear but Ninji outsmarted Derick.

Instead of coming from out of the sun, like Derick had anticipated, Ninji used the reverberations from the surrounding Island to make a deadly pass at Derick's back. It almost worked. However, Derick, had detected a shift in the air pressure behind him and had spun suddenly, ducked, and had raised his staff, striking out. Derick's eyes were focused on the giant Hummingbird as it passed, inches from where he stood.

In a heartbeat, Ninji stopped, his wings fanning, creating an ear shattering cataclysm of hurricane force pressure. Derick was trying to hold his ground, but the forces were too great, and he had to retreat to the caves entrance. Safely shielded by the rocky entrance, Derick turned, looking at the demonic Hummingbird.

Ninji advancing, daring Derick to face him—their eyes locking…

"Yes!" Derick thought, even though he could see the fury in Ninji's eyes. And Ninji's eyes were drinking in Derick's fear, treasuring every moment. Ninji's eyes were, in fact, a wild gold, with a glowing sliver of burnt orange. The menace was obvious, furious in degrees, but there was a hint of weakness. Derick just about missed that look but when he did, his reaction was quick.

Derick suddenly lunged, swinging his staff violently at Ninji; the blow was parried by his beak.

Ninji readjusted his angle of attack and swiftly began another engagement. Back and forth it went—whack, whack, a satisfying stalemate. Each one eager in the battlement. And Ninji backed off for a heartbeat, adjusting his flight with ease and advanced.

Derick's only option was to back up slowly with cautious steps and stave off any blows and continued to seek any opening. The fight was finally broken when Ninji opened his beak, parried a series of blows, then; his tongue was lashing out, striking Derick soundly. The lick started near Derick's chin and traveled over his cheek and into his hair. Yes! Ninji performed the Hummingbird's kiss, perfectly...

"EEWWWW..." Derick screamed, backing away slowly—his staff raised high with one hand, easily defending every blow. He responded with surprised delight, because the wood was reacting without him thinking, which amazed him. The Hummingbird's kiss had restored more fight and vigor than he thought possible. Derick knew every move Ninji was going to perform. This encouraged Derick to fight smarter, and he felt nirvana.

Meanwhile, his other hand was tracing the spot of where the kiss had landed—wiping, feeling for any blood seeping out of a cut, his feelings were a mixed blessing of disgust and honor. So many emotions were flooding through him, scenarios flashing past brightly but the adrenalin was intoxicating: driving him past his breaking point; but then it dawned on Derick and he realized the secret. And with that though; he broke it off, stepped back quickly into the cave's safety. Derick's mind recording every little motion that Ninji was making.

However, while Derick was retreating. Ninji was advancing, eyes ablaze; he hovered in one spot for half a second, shifted, and in another second, changed to another angle. Finally, Ninji, with his head held high began emitting his faithful whistle and was gone. And the Island remained quiet.

Derick was soaked in sweat, sucking in vast quantities of air, but— felt so... invigorated. He tried to relax: pacing back and forth while taking deep cleansing breaths; slowing his heart rate, calming his nerves; he lowered his staff, exhaustion causing him to collapse.

Miko was by his side: catching him with ease; her arms encircled him in a gentle embrace. She gently lowered him to the ground, her hands exploring, comforting. Her fingers slowly traced slow circles over his lips and she stared into his eyes. Her eyes gleamed with excitement. She was rocking him, a smile playing on her lips and she whispered, "Ninji likes you!"

"That though crossed my mind after he licked me with that tongue. Man! That felt so weird, but…" he trailed off; lost in thought, appreciating her concern. Minutes passed and in a whisper, he asked, "Do you know where Ninji's nest is?"

"Yes! But…?" Miko replied with a silent nod of her head, her eyes closing slowly in half, tears building, her head starting to drop in defeat.

Derick reacted quickly, one of his hands shooting out, tenderly, cupping her chin with one finger, softly, under her chin and his thumb caressing her lips. He lifted her head, making eye contact and his other hand, rising gently, brushing her tears away. So many emotions were passing between them; no words were necessary and each one communicating with an intimate reading of minds.

Derick closed his eyes, leaned in, lips poised…

"Not yet! We need to finish this, pleasure later…!" Miko whispered in a soft, sexy tone…

Derick groaned, he tried to control the passion but…

Minutes later after they had adjusted their clothing, hand in hand, they were stepping out…

Derick murmuring, "That charm? If it was to be broken…?"

Miko smiled her answer and Derick felt confident.

Miko led the way into the green morass of a dense jungle with silent steps. Their eyes sharp: catching minute details; hearing whispers of warnings from each giant plant they stepped past.

Derick's eyes were drinking in the experience. So many exotic flowers; bigger than his mind could comprehend. Sure, he had seen flowers as big as dinner plates but these on this Island were on a colossal scale. All earth real specters of the color chart exploding: mingling; and the scents intoxicating. They moved as one in silence, and…

Miko suddenly came to a dead stop, holding up her hand, pointing at her ear, then her eyes, "We are in Ninji's feeding grounds! Look sharp?" She whispered, her eyes saying—be cautious. Derick responded by reaching out: caressing her arm in understanding.

Miko made a strange but brilliant maneuver; she grasped one of the succulent, sweet fragrance flower, pulled with all her might, shaking the flower, violently.

The flower: under the onslaught; released an avalanche of pollen, raining down over Miko and covering her in a fine mist. Derick understood instantly, mimicking her actions, shaking another flower with gusto and he, too, was covered by the fine mist. Derick resisted for a few seconds, but... he managed to muffle his sneezes.

Derick's mind was reeling: so, sweet... blending with the flower; feeling its strength, its potential, he was giddy with excitement. These thoughts were affecting him and he so wanted to strip and run free. But before he could react to this temptation...

And without warning, Ninji had stopped directly over head of Derick.

Ninji's wings were beating fast and he flew with style. His colors were bright, a deep green on the body. The violet sparkling around his neck. His tail adjusting with each body movement. Closer and closer Ninji drifting down, aligning himself with the flower—his beak penetrated the flower, he started to feed.

And the charm, shining brightly, swinging freely, so close...so tantalizing...

Derick struck fast—dead on target; he could hear the charm crack. However, before he could make another strike, Ninji was shooting up out of range, enraged. His wings beating, multiplied ten-fold, his eyes ablaze and he was glancing around: trying to sight a target.

Derick stood frozen, his staff gripped firmly in one hand and before he could make another strike...

Miko had tackled him. Laying him out flat. She was on top of him, her hair splayed out and her body hiding them.

Ninji hovered overhead, his flight off. He shook violently for a few seconds, then, with an angry chirp, he was gone.

Derick felt so—content: he knew that the surprising blow had struck home! He knew... it had affected Ninji, weakening him: making him—careless. Anticipation surging over every one of his nerve endings. His muscles contracted; adrenaline pumped through his veins. His heart beating wildly, with purpose—one goal on his mind...but...

Derick blew out a heavy, deep breath, enjoying this moment of intimacy with Miko.

"I cracked the charm!" Derick whispered into Miko's ear.

She shuddered and replied, softly, "I know! I heard it, too!"

They lay together, bonding, relieved, but...hesitant. A relief of joy was spreading, making both of them relax, the pleasure —and, a closing of a chapter.

Miko and Derick approached in silence.

Ninji was resting in his nest, his eyes closed. His beak was open and his black tongue sticking out. The broken charm was dangling loosely around his colossal neck.

Derick was holding his breath, gathering his nerves and struck fast. He had unsheathed his yellow dive knife, placed a death grip around the handle, rotating the stainless-steel blade away from Ninji's body and struck the charm, dead on, with the knives steel handle, a shattering death blow.

The charm sizzled; breaking into many pieces, pouring out a white light of intense power. The light was blinding Derick at once; but a peaceful joy of accomplishment flooded throughout his body and soul and his mind at ease with fulfillment.

Ninji reacted instantly—taking flight. His wings beating franticly; fast and furious and pummeled Derick about his head.

Derick felt the fatal strike and he felt like a leaf blowing through the air, spinning, swirling, on a never ending cycle of wind that carried him up—up—and —falling... falling... darkness encompassing his vision but the smile on his face was electrifying.

Derick's consciousness returned; he tried to open his eye, they felt heavy and sore with a pounding headache, too, just like a hangover. He took deep breaths, in doing so; he could smell the sea with that sweet salty tang which was invigorating.

The Island's fragrances were a faint memory. This baffled him momentarily and he groaned. He tried to sit up: the pain was intense; dizziness sweeping over every nerve ending, he shut his eyes, tightly, and reached for his head.

"You're on your sailboat! But...how in the world? And were under sail power, too?" The sailboats movements were registering in his fogged mind. But the spinning was boring into his soul; causing him to grimace, clasping his fingers around the bunk's wood frame. Ever so slowly, between deep breaths, he forced his eyes open to confirm he was, indeed, on his sailboat. He was making mental notes. "Nothing seemed broken, but... How did I...?"

He wanted to shout for joy, but, that was painful, too. So he waited, feeling his strength returning. He sat up, his mind protesting but he fought through the light headedness and sat quietly on the bunk. He closed his eyes, listening, gathering more energy and finally... he stood. This sudden movement, however, was forcing him to reach out, both hands slapping against a bulk head, to steady him, but he stood on rubbery legs, the queasiness passing, and... he was marching to the cabin's door. And with a strong twist of the wrist, a push from a hand, the door was flung open, with force.

He stepped onto the sailboats open deck: breathing in the intense, salty air, feeling the wind rustling his hair, and, as he turned to the tiller... he froze. He drew in a deep breath.

Miko stood, hands on the helm, her legs planted wide apart, ridding the movements of the sailboat natural rhythm with a steady, graceful ease. Her long dark hair, acting as a flag on the stiff breeze with a few stray strands camouflaging her face. She simply brushed them away, tucking the runaways behind her ear.

She turned, hearing his intake of breath, her smile was intoxicating. Within a second her eyes became alive when they made contact with his. Her sigh of relief was wicked and she motioned to Derick by patting a seat. Derick's smile was of total acceptance.

And on her shoulder, Ninji was perched; just for a second, because, when their eyes met Ninji decided to take wing. He hovered an inch above Miko's shoulder, emitting his whistle of hello. As Ninji settled down, lightly landing on Miko's shoulder. He performed his body and wing shakes with a little wiggle and an intense stare. Derick missed that flash of orange which flashed in Ninji's eyes for a Nano second. Ninji's beak opened and his tongue came out and he wiggled that black tongue at Derick, who smiled. Ninji was back to his pre-demonic form.

Derick blew out a deep breath, stepping fast and graceful to where she was and sat down with a groan, reaching for her hand.

Miko watched him for a few seconds, her smile bright and with a hearty laugh of delight; she turned her head and looked to the horizon. One hand lightly on the helm, she replied, coyly, "Later, when you're stronger! I have a story to tell you."

Richard A. Wentworth

Me and my family live in the Southern California desert and when I'm not working, I like to write and create interesting stories.
www.facebook.com/susan.wentworth.7

The Legend of Chucacabra

By Jeremy Rodden

We all gathered around the bonfire for one last storytelling session before we left Camp Westoria for home sections of Toonopolis. The experience was one to remember for those of us from areas of our cartoon city that didn't remotely resemble the American Old West like this one. I made great friends hailing from diverse corners of Toonopolis such as Camenot, Pixelburgh, Supercity, and Steamport. My own home, Animetown, was almost as far from Westoria as a section of Toonopolis could be.

After all the horseback riding, story swapping, gun shooting, and trail hiking, we would sit at the bonfire eating our evening meal (tonight it was hamburgers) and listen to a story told by Wayne Northwood, the oldest and most respected guide/cowboy in all Westoria. That last night, Wayne made it clear he saved his most chilling story for last.

"Let me tell yer," Wayne began, instantly silencing the murmurs around the bonfire, "I done saved my most chilling story for last." His weather-worn eyes creased even further into a far-off gaze as he stared through us all and into the darkness behind us. He ran his hand through his white, frontiersman beard in a sagely fashion. His voice was slightly muffled by the wad of chewing tobacco he always kept tucked in his left cheek.

"This is the Legend of the Chucacabra."

He allowed for silent reverie at the title. There were whispers among the campers but the crackling of wood in the bonfire dominated the airwaves.

"Don't you mean Poopacabra?" asked the sarcastic sidekick from Supercity, Plucky McGee.

A death glare from Wayne silenced the snark instantly. Time at Camp Westoria, especially at the shooting range, made everyone at camp respect Wayne's eagle-eyed stare. If he drew on us, nothing we could do would stop him from gunning us down. I was pretty sure he'd never actually do it, but I also was pretty sure I didn't want to find out if he would.

"The Legend of the Chucacabra," he said again through gritted teeth. This time, no one interrupted him and our hushed silence grew even deeper. We settled in and prepared for Wayne's story. The way he told his stories would transport us directly into them, almost as if we were framed inside the story within our own story.

"Some say the Chucacabra haunts Westoria to this day. But it wasn't always a demonically possessed creature of death and destruction, no sir. As the story goes, it was once a regular coyote, prowling the desert hills of Westoria just like any other coyote would do: hunt at night, sleep during the day, and stay away from people. Quite misanthropic, coyotes."

He tossed a grin to Missy, our friend from Steamport whose full name was Misanthrope Beechworth. She fidgeted with her goggles nervously. He continued, "One coyote, however, grew bolder. You see, as human settlements encroached into the wilderness more and more, the coyote's habitat shrank more and more. For most of the coyotes, this meant they decreased their range to continue staying away from people. This clever coyote, however, began to embrace the humans and realized that among the wastefulness and destruction of humankind could be found free food.

You see, hunting is hard work, cowboys and cowgirls, as you've come to learn in your stay at Camp Westoria. Why buy the horse when you can get the meat for free, after all?"

A sound of disgust went up from the gathered campers, who were either looking at their plates of food, clutching their stomachs, or on the verge of vomiting into the bonfire. I personally felt no problem with the idea that we were eating horsemeat. *Basashi* was not an uncommon dish in Animetown, after all. I guessed the rest of my campmates weren't as keen on the idea. I shrugged and took another bite of my hamburger (or horseburger).

"Oh settle down, you daisies," Wayne spat. "It's just a saying. You're eating cow, not horse."

Several of the campers looked relieved. A few still looked at their plates of food side-eyed and were clearly done eating for the night.

Wayne Northwood smiled his wry smile, suggesting his choice of words was not an accident but simply a gag he liked to play on the campers. I found this easy to believe because the man never said something he didn't mean to say. Even if he did, he made it so easy to feel like it was on purpose that it might have well been.

"You see, campers, before humans moved in on the coyote territory, the coyotes would hunt rabbits, rodents, and even larger game like deer and bison. They'd even go after small birds."

A sound went up from an unidentified camper and Wayne Northwood held up his hand immediately to silence the question he could tell was coming.

"Now afore you all go off on that famous coyote and roadrunner situation, let me stop you. We live in a world of fact, even in the Tooniverse. Some of you may come from some pretty fantastical sections of Toonopolis." He pointed to me and said, "Yuki there comes from a really wacky part without a lot of grounding in reality."

I wasn't sure to take offense or to agree with him. Sure, Animetown seemed perfectly normal if it was all you ever knew, but having travelled to other sections of the Tooniverse, I knew it was pretty far on the absurd end of the spectrum at times. Even so, I felt I should defend my home section so I stuck out my tongue and took my right index finger to my lower right eyelid and pulled it down.

"Don't you *akanbe* me, son," the cowboy said immediately.

I quickly pulled in my tongue and released my eyelid. Not only did he see me through the fire and smoke, he even knew what my expression was called in Japanese. There really wasn't getting anything past this old man. I looked down at my feet.

"And don't none of the rest of you think about eyeballin' me or sassin', ya hear? I thought you all done learned that by now." He cleared his throat. "As I were sayin', in Westoria we are grounded in the grit and reality of life. This here section of Toonopolis is firmly rooted in the American Old West, myself included.

Now in the real world, a roadrunner is no match racing a coyote, even without all them fancy gizmos and gadgets. A roadrunner can only reach a top speed of twenty miles per hour while a coyote can get up to nearly forty-five miles per hour. Of course, roadrunners can fly so they wouldn't try to outrun a coyote in the first place, they'd just fly away. So leave all that nonsense out of your heads.

Now this one coyote decided he was gonna take the easy road and start scavenging off the human civilization moving in around them. Why chase a rabbit or fight with a cobra when the humans would just leave piles of food in containers right next to their buildings? Luckily for this coyote, he never ate anything he wasn't supposed to eat and get hisself sick. Unluckily, though, he got something far worse."

He took a deep breath and paused for effect.

"One day while he was foraging out back of a Generic Offbrand Mexican Restaurant, he stumbled across something that tore apart his insides—"

"Right?" Plucky McGee interrupted. "That stuff really goes through me, too."

A gunshot went off before any of us even saw any movement. The stool where the sidekick from Supercity was sitting collapsed under him and he tumbled to the ground hard. I watched him get to his feet, dust himself off, and look at the stool that was now missing a leg. I followed my eyes back to Wayne Northwood, who was holding his six-shooter. The gun had a thin tendril of smoke coming out of the barrel.

"I done warned you, kid," he said.

"I can't help it!" Plucky responded. "I'm a superhero sidekick. I have to make the sarcastic poop jokes. It's in my nature."

Wayne nodded, "That's why the bullet hit your chair instead of you. Or did you think I missed?"

Plucky shook his head violently. None of us would have thought he missed. Wayne Northwood never missed. Plucky tried to put his stool back together but quickly realized that a two-legged stool that was supposed to have three legs was not very useful as a seat anymore. He sighed and sat in the dirt instead.

Wayne seemed satisfied with Plucky's punishment and continued, "Now when I say insides, I don't mean the coyote's guts." He paused and glared at Plucky, who made a 'mouth zipped' motion with his hand across his lips. "I mean the soul of the coyote. You see: there is a nasty little type of demon that likes to frequent Mexican restaurants called a Caca Demon. This demon likes to hide itself among the heat and spices so you don't taste it.

To humans, a Caca Demon is mostly harmless. Like Mr. McGee said a few moments ago, they contribute to the food 'going right through you'

I believe were his words." He looked at Plucky, who nodded. "A Caca Demon only takes a tiny bit of your soul on the way through. This is why people will often feel really bad after a big Mexican fast food meal. Well, that and the flaming diarrhea."

Several people laughed. A few people looked around to see if they were allowed to laugh. It was hard to tell if Wayne was joking or serious because he always was so stern. Of course, he did make jokes from time to time and it seemed he liked to torture us into trying to figure out if laughter was appropriate. It appeared to be okay in this case because none of the laughers got scolded. By the time we sorted it out, though, the moment had passed and the humor was gone. Thus was the beautiful irony of a Wayne Northwood joke.

"As I was sayin'," he said, casting another glare at Plucky, "the Caca Demon is mostly harmless to us. But to a coyote, well, no one ever knew what one would do until it did.

One night, not unlike tonight, a worker at the Generic Offbrand Mexican Restaurant was clearin' out the trash at the end of his shift and heard a rustlin' by the trashcans. The boy assumed it was just a round tailed squirrel or a rabbit, desert critters that would often eat the leftover greens or insects around the trash. What he found there was something else entirely."

Wayne once again paused for dramatic effect. He let his eyes sweep the gathered campers and then spit out of the corner of his mouth and continued. "What that young man found all them years ago was a coyote. But he could tell right away that this was no ordinary coyote. Your average Westoria coyote, as you know, is about three to four feet long with a foot, foot-and-a-half long tail. This creature shared that with the coyote it once was, but that was about it.

Where it once had fur, the animal had dry, scaly looking skin. Its eyes were sunken in and red as a bottle of Tabasco sauce. Its spine and tail were distorted, curved up almost like the four-legged beast was trying to become a two-legged creature. Along the ridges of its spine were four to five-inch-long spikes that looked like they grew right out of the vertebrae. Its lips were nearly non-existent, pulled back to reveal even bigger and sharper fangs than any coyote should possess.

And when this young man realized he was staring at a monster, he did what any good Westoria boy would do."

Wayne took a pause and looked around. It seemed like he was looking for a response from someone but no one spoke up. So I asked, "What was that?"

Wayne removed his gun from its holster with his lightning-quick draw and pointed it at me, "He shot at the bastard with his six-shooter, o' course."

"Did he hit it?" I followed, while moving my head slightly to the side to no longer be in the sights of his gun.

Wayne smiled coyly and slipped his gun back into the holster smoothly. "Yer damn right he did." He punctuated the statement with a spit of his chewing tobacco into the fire. A pungent puff of smoke curled out from where he spat.

"But it didn't do jack squat to the beast. The former coyote screeched at him and fell back to four legs after a shot hit him squarely in the side. In a regular coyote, it would have been a direct strike to the heart and left him dead instantly. In this creature, a foul-smelling black ooze came from the wound and left a trail of liquid crap like it had dysentery as it fled back into the desert."

"Crap?" Missy asked.

"They might call it night soil where you're from, Missy. Feces, excrement," Wayne paused and looked at Plucky McGee, who looked like he was going to burst from keeping his comments to himself any longer. "Go ahead, Plucky."

"POOOOOOOOOP!" Plucky shouted from his place on the dirt ground.

"I see," Missy replied. "Thank you, sir."

"Why can't you be more proper like her, Plucky?" Wayne asked.

"Because she's from snooty Steamport and I'm from Supercity?" he replied.

"I'll have you know," Missy began once again fiddling with the goggles around her neck, "that being polite and proper knows no bounds, regardless of status or upbringing."

Plucky rolled his eyes. This was a common exchange I'd observed between my two friends over the course of camp. No matter what happened next, neither would budge from their position so they learned to just stop before it turned into an hours-long debate. The rest of us were quite appreciative when they figured this out.

"So the creature left a trail of *unpi*?" I asked, trying to get the story back on course.

"That it did, Yuki," Wayne replied. "Liquid stool from the trashcans back to the desert. The young man wanted to track the creature and finish the job, but he had to finish wiping down the prep stations in the restaurant and did not want to be derelict to his duties.

After that night, other reports began pouring in around Westoria about the foul creature that once was a coyote. Anyone who was able to land a shot on the beast reported the same reviling ooze in place of blood. And it seemed to heal from the wounds immediately, the ooze plugging the hole and keeping the critter alive, no matter how badly injured.

This is where the creature earned its nickname: Chucacabra. It derived its name from the Chupacabra, a legend of Latin America in the Real World, but you know, with poop inside of it."

Plucky let out a loud guffaw. I was afraid Wayne was going to shoot at him again and, this time there was no stool for him to shoot out instead.

Luckily, Wayne just shrugged and said, "I don't disagree Plucky. But I weren't the one to name it. But the name stuck with the dimwit locals and there you have it. And that, boys and girls, is the Legend of the Chucacabra."

A round of disappointment came from the gathered campers. A few of them even started booing and crying out complaints.

"What do you mean?"

"How is that all?"

"Lame!"

"What happened to it?" I added to the cacophony.

Wayne held up a hand to silence us and it was quite effective. "Now now, kids. One at a time." He pointed to a squire-looking kid from Camenot whose name I forget.

"Sir Wayne," he began.

"I told you before, I ain't no sir," Wayne responded tersely.

"Yes, sorry, sir. Um, I mean, Mr. Wayne. But how is that the entirety of the story? What happened to it?" the squire asked earnestly. I was glad he stole my question so I could stay quiet.

"Nothing," the cowboy said.

"What the hell?" Plucky spat out.

Wayne's eyes flew open wide and he stared at Plucky. "Hell indeed, Mr. McGee. Because some say that's where the demon creature fled to after being hunted by so many ranchers and restaurant owners for trespassing and eating their livestock and trash."

The campers settled back down, realizing Wayne was not really done but was just baiting them.

"The sheriff rounded a posse of folk willing to head into the desert to track the beast, but they couldn't find him. One day, reports of the Chucacabra just stopped coming in and the fear died down. Some say it finally died of its wounds. Some say it fled to another section of Toonopolis. Still others, myself included, say it returned to the hell from whence the Caca Demon originally came and waits for the perfect moment to return to the surface and feed once again."

The campsite devolved once again to complete silence save the crackling of the bonfire. The campers all looked at each other and around into the darkness of the desert around them. Several of us inched our stools closer to the fire and away from the darkness. The gleam in Wayne Northwood's eye suggested he knew exactly what he was doing with the way he told the story. Plucky raised his hand tentatively.

Wayne made eye contact with him and nodded. "Mr. Northwood, how do we know this story isn't full of as much caca as the coyote?" He asked the question seriously but clearly his word selection wasn't the best. That was Plucky for you.

The cowboy reached into the C-space behind him and pulled out a purple visor. It was really old and worn and the faded yellow letters on the front read "Generic Offbrand Mexican Restaurant" in fancy script. "Because, Mr. McGee," he said while removing his cowboy hat and placing the visor over his long gray hair, "I was that young worker who was the first to spy the creature and strike the first blow."

The campers gasped, ooh'ing and aah'ing at the revelation. Plucky was left dumbstruck. I wasn't sure if Wayne was telling the truth or just playing out a longer ruse, but it sure was convincing and we had learned never to be too surprised at the things Wayne has seen and done in his long years. Suffice to say, though, we all had a little trouble sleeping that last night in camp, wondering if every sound we heard in the desert around us might be the Chucacabra, returning from hell to feast once again.

Jeremy Rodden

Jeremy Rodden considers himself a dad first and an author second. He is the author of the middle grade/young adult Toonopolis series of books which take place in his cartoon universe. He also edited, contributed to, and published The Myth of Mr. Mom, a non-fiction series of essays by stay-at- home dads.

www.toonopolis.com
www.facebook.com/toonopolisfiles
www.twitter.com/toonopolis
www.amazon.com/Jeremy-Rodden/e/B00515J2LC

CATagories for 500

By Clint Doyle

The man sat on his couch. His butt creaked under the cracked, black pleather as he settled in for some day-time television. His soaps wouldn't be on for another hour so he had microwaved his usual chicken pot pie lunch and popped the tab on a diet sprite and settled in for his normal routine as Alex Trebeck took the podium to introduce this round of contestants.

A sharp scuttling noise nearly made him choke on a mouthful of luke-warm carrots (the center never got warm like it should). A dark bolt tore out of the kitchen scrabbling across the floor and under the curtain. What the hell made cats do that anyway? At least it had stop shredding the chair next to his bed.

Warwick peered out from under the curtain. His prey had eluded him. It had probably crossed over into the mirrored realm through the convenient glass door which isolated his hunting ground from the World Beyond. The Nybbas was nothing more than a minor nuisance spirit. No real issue here, but he would be skinned before he just let some low rent haunter waltz into his domain.

Since the time before humans built the pyramids, cats have guarded them against the encroachment of the spirit world. Their dual existence in both the Human world and the Spirit Realm made them natural guardians.

Warwick made his way from behind the curtains, throwing a casual glance over his shoulder to the glass door to ensure the reflective surface had indeed closed the passage to the world that lived behind the mirrors. He sauntered up to his Human charge. This was not his first. In fact, this was his 7th. Two more to go and he could take his place as an Oracle in the collective consciousness. Cats held the memories not only of their past lives, but the collected wisdom of their whole species.

Sitting next to Cheeto, that was what he called his current charge, he began his midday ritual of cleaning his jet-black fur. Once completed, he would get to the serious business of his midday nap. Cheeto was engrossed in the program from the box which trapped the souls of other stupid humans. From his considerable estimation, anyone that got stuck in that box was deserving of their fate judging by the drivel that they produced. He missed the days when people read books. At least this show featured the torment of those too stupid to know even basic facts. He yawned and narrowed his eyes at Cheeto. His current charge looked like he would be right at home embarrassing himself in front of the white-haired demon tormenting the trapped souls. Warwick knew him for a demon, he can see the delight in his eyes as the humans fumbled for his amusement. Cheeto was lucky though. Warwick was not about to suffer the humiliation of letting his charge be consumed by the flickering box.

As the show progressed, Warwick noticed a shift in the atmosphere, another presence had entered his domain. Warwick looked around quickly taking in the scene looking for danger.

Cheeto for his part put his hand on his head and stroked him. "What is wrong with you?"

Warwick rose lithely to his feet and left his charge in safety on the couch. "Of course, you get my attention then wander off, ungrateful cat."

Warwick ignored Cheeto and zeroed in on the source of his unease. There, turned on its side, sat a box from the Amazon. Why the people from there mailed Cheeto things he would never understand, but that was a thought for another time. He rushed the box in a mad dash to catch whatever had invaded his territory. The box rocked, scooted back several feet from the force of his charge. In the Spirit realm though, Warwick shot his claws into the darkness snaring the intruder.

He thrust his head into the box to see what he had caught. No minor apparition this. He found himself holding nothing short of a Nephilim! What was this doing here?

Warwick challenged the demon. "Halt, and by the Accord give your name or be forever banished!"

A voice like frozen malice returned to him. "I am known as Rhudduryyg, asked and answered, with my Right I declare myself Free and Sovereign. Now release me Guardian."

"I am no kitten, and that was shameful for you to even suggest it might work. I have you and may do as I please unless you care to make offering. Why did you invade my realm?"

The demon growled the sound of cracking ice, but Warwick did not budge his claws. The demon tried to slide back to the underworld through the shadows inside the box. Warwick held on and dug in with his hind legs, kicking and digging into the box.

Cheeto heard the scuffling. He looked toward Warwick with consternation. *Don't worry,* thought Warwick, *this one will not escape his due. He will not harm you. Humans were always so anxious.*

"Damn you, feline," the demon roared, "release me!"

"Isn't that sort of an ironic turn of phrase for your kind? Anyhow, you are bound, and I will not release you until I have your intentions for my charge." With the condition set, Warwick released the demon's essence. He began to clean his paws of the oily essence of the creature with his tongue in order to emphasize to the demon his control of the situation. Cheeto glanced away from his show to notice he had the situation well in hand. He returned the human a flat stare, as if there were any other possibility.

"Fine, if I tell you will you let me go?"

"Perhaps," purred Warwick, "if the reason is good enough."

"I came to taint his seed. The boss down-under expects this one to sire a lineage with excellent potential for being Fated. Figures if we get in on the ground floor, in a few generations we can claim first rights on any who might be of value."

Hmm, boss demons thought Cheeto here had something special in his pants? Man, where did they get their intel? If Cheeto ever found a mate, Warwick would be so surprised he may return to the collective out of sheer surprise.

"What aren't you telling me?" Warwick sensed deception, typical with this lot now that he thought about it. "If you are holding out on me so help me I will tip this box over and expose you to the daylight." The full light of day would see this jerk banished back to Hell for at least a year. That is, if his superiors didn't hold him there a millennia to torture him for failure.

"You asked, I answered! Now release me." The demon tried to retreat but was bound fast by the compact with Warwick. He was going nowhere until Warwick let him. The push of the demon against his bonds was enough to tip the box over trapping Warwick underneath. Not wanting to be stuck in such close proximity to this foul creature, he began to buck. After a few attempts, he managed to extricate himself from within the cardboard serving as the demon's prison. Cheeto was glaring at the box. Did he sense the foulness of the monster inside? Maybe he did, but he turned back to the game and left the matter to Warwick.

"As I was saying," Warwick began to paw at the edge of the box, lifting it slightly, "what aren't you saying?"

"Go to hell!"

Warwick pawed harder, and the box began to lift. "Do you understand what I will do to you if you stick your hand under here again? The fury I can unleash in the mortal world." He batted the top corner, the edge came up a few inches.

"Fine! Just stop with the sunlight thing!"

"I'm waiting." Warwick sang, which of course came out as a series of meows as he circled the box.

Cheeto eyed him with a strange look. Humans really were so dense. Warwick really began to wonder if this one could manage to get enough food to support himself if he ran out of those amazing pies that came out of the Ding Machine. Perhaps he would kill a mouse or something and offer it to Cheeto as an invitation to come hunting. A matter for another time. The demon was speaking.

"How about this? We play for it. You win, I spill the beans. I win, you let me out of here and about my business. What do you say, feline?"

Warwick stretched out his paw, the claws sinking into the carpet. As he examined the space between his claws, casually he said, "I accept, and as the challenged I get to determine the contest."

"Done. A deal is struck." Warwick felt the Accord's binding settle in. "What sort of contest do you choose?"

He twitched his whiskers, "Oh I don't care. This is just to make you feel better about yourself." Warwick sighed and glanced at Cheeto. He was totally engrossed in his program. He considered the flicking machine and the deception it contained. "Heh, I will even beat you at your own game, Demon. I choose Jeopardy. We take turns. Most right answers wins."

"Very well, Cat," the demon replied, his voice sinister and intent upon the game.

"Looking at the board we have only one category left. James, you have control." The sinister host taunted his victim. "Beyonce for 400 Alex!" the contestant quavered.

"In an SNL skit, Justin Timberlake and Andy Samberg, in leotards and heels, replaced Bey's female dancers in this video."

"What is, All the Single Ladies?", snapped the Demon.

"All the Single Ladies," confirmed Trebeck. Warwick yawned.

Beyonce for 200. "Before she was an independent woman, Beyonce was part of this group that hit with 'Independent Women Part 1," droned the host.

"Who is Destiny's Child?" Warwick replied with no hesitation.

"Correct." The host voiced to a contestant who also knew the answer.

One of the contestants spoke out, "Beyonce for 1000!"

Trebeck immediately fired back, "In the movie Cadillac Records, Beyonce played this R&B legend and sang "At Last" on the soundtrack."

The human hesitated. The demon responded, "Who is Dianne Reeves?"

"Who is 'Dianne Reeves?'" the human confirmed, and both were rewarded with the buzz of an incorrect response.

"Who is Etta James?" purred Warwick. Time expired and Trebeck confirmed his answer. The next contestant selected his dollar amount. "No one loves Bey more," the cat taunted.

"Answer, Jay Z is featured on this Beyonce song that mentions 'That liquor get into me'," queried Trebeck.

"Drunk in Love," cat and creature replied. "That one is mine!" howled the damned soul, "You got the last one". Warwick hissed and Cheeto threw the empty can of soda just over Warwick's head and at the box. The human mumbled something, but Warwick countered to the demon. "The answer is mine. You missed yours. The rules allow me to steal, and this one is mine. I am ahead by two."

A strange beep played over the speaker and Trebeck informed the contestants that only one question remained and began to review their totals. Warwick bared his teeth. He had won.

The demon must have sensed his satisfaction and replied in a voice close to panic, "Wait! The final question! We are allowed to wage! You must let me wager!"

Warwick climbed on top of the box and looked over the edge. "What could you possibly bet? There is no scenario where you win this. Give over. It is time to fess up."

"I wager a weekly delivery of canned fish."

Warwick stopped, very still and quiet he said, "You can't possibly deliver on that."

Frantic, the demon elaborated, "Deliver, exactly. A mistake in the system for at least a month. We have that kind of pull. You know we do. Odds are better that even he feeds you the fish."

Trebeck had finished totaling each contest and announced. "Today's Final Jeopardy category is Ancient Egypt."

Warwick leaped from the box in triumph. With his collective memory, he couldn't possibly lose. He could almost taste the fish, but that was a far cry from the true prize. He crowed, "You know I would have done it for just the empty boxes, but this is going to be great. I will bet Ol' Cheeto's soul here. There absolutely nothing they can ask that I can't answer. You are going to pay for this when you get back down there." This of course came out as the most pleasurable of yowls and the ante was upped.

There was no response from the box, just a sense of utter defeat. Warwick sat up and waited for the commercials to conclude, pleased with himself to no end.

Cheeto got up, but instead of putting his dishes in the sink where Warwick could lick them clean for him later, he moved decisively towards the demon's hiding place. What was he doing? He was going to ruin this. Warwick yowled and batted his paws trying to warn Cheeto.

"Damn cat, you are not going to ruin my stories for me," the human declared as he scooped up the cat. "You can wait for Oprah in here." And in one quick motion, Cheeto opened the door and tossed Warwick upon the bed and promptly shut the door. There he sat, far away from the TV and the game. He began to yowl, to protest, to raise hell to save Cheeto. Then the indignity of his begging caught up with him and he thought, "You deserve this." He guessed that he would have to wait a bit longer before taking his place as an Oracle. He curled up and went to sleep with no trouble at all.

Clint Doyle

Clint Doyle is a new author with interest in Fantasy, Urban Fantasy, and Steampunk. He lives in Dallas, Texas with his wife and four children. He is working on his first major production currently.

Antichrist is a Manatee

By Valerie Willis

L ittle Suzie skipped through the cool darkness, humming happily to herself. She followed the carpeted pathway down further into the cave-like room. Barely seen on the walls were the fake embellishments of rocks, plants and even the occasional hint of freshwater fish. She skipped ever deeper into the cavern towards the dim light up ahead, her excitement growing. Her humming had stopped and she now walked with widening eyes as the blue ambience filled them ever more. She stumbled to a stop in front on the center large acrylic window.

"Come closer, Child."

The creepy voice made her look over her shoulder. Nothing seemed notable but the dark corridor and the blinding brightness of the entrance; no one else was here. She had left her parents behind at the door as they sat on a bench, relishing the air conditioning just inside the attraction. They had encouraged her to venture alone, to *take your time* so that they might recoup from the searing heat outside. Seeing no signs of anyone else joining her adventure, she turned back to the viewing window.

"Oh!" She gasped.

There before her hovered a massive heap of grey flesh. She giggled as he reminded her of an enormous grey potato with whiskers. A frown crossed her lips; manatees weren't as exciting as everyone had made them out to be. The whiskers twitched and a few bubbles rolled out of the nostrils on his squishy round muzzle. Its beady little eyes rolled to peer down at her, as if disappointed in how tiny she was in comparison to himself.

"Will you join me, Child?" Again, the mysterious voice.

Suzie swung herself around, but once more, found she was alone in the blue glow of the aquarium window.

"H-hello?" Her tiny voice echoed as she squinted at the dark corners of the room and corridor.

"No, Child. Behind you." A thumping brought her back around to stare at the manatee who had moved closer to the window.

A smile crawled across her little freckled face. Excited that the grey potato was so close, she too joined him. Her nose pressed firmly against the acrylic made her look like a pig from the manatee's side. Now she could count the whiskers in his snout, see the rolls and folds of grey flesh that made her giggle to see he had not one, but four chins adorning his neck. He flapped a fin, thumping the window and she jumped back. After a shocked pause, she laughed and ran back to the manatee. With a hardy slap, she high-fived her new potato friend.

"Stop that!" Bubbles rolled from the manatee's nostrils. "I command you to stop your buffoonery at once!"

"You can talk!" She gasped, clapping her hands excitedly. "No one told me manatees could talk!"

Another snort of bubbles, "Do you know who stands before you, Child?"

Blinking, she pulled at a curly strand of her auburn hair. "Mister Manatee?"

The tiny bulgy eyes started to glow red as he thumped the window with both flippers. "I am the Antichrist!"

"The what?" She furrowed her brow. "The Ann, the anteee, I can call you Andy!"

"NO!" Bubbles exploded from his snout this time.

Suzie laughed, clapping excitedly, "BUBBLES!"

Suddenly the potato floated up and away. Smashing herself against the window she watched in wonder. He had such a big circular fin, unlike the dolphins and whales she had seen in the other dark rooms. With a cheek firm against the cool acrylic, she looked upward, watching as he took in a gulp of air. Slowly he drifted back down to her level again where she smiled warmly, happy her new friend had returned. This was a rather slow process, taking several minutes for the massive mammal to achieve as if a snail climbing up and back down a sliding glass door.

"You're funny!" She was tugging on her shirt and swinging her body from side-to-side.

"Hmph." Again, he peered down at her as if a King staring at the homeless. "Again, I ask, will you follow me, Child?"

"Umm, where are we going?" Content that her conversation would be continuing she sat on the floor. "I'll have to ask Mommy and Daddy if it's ok to go with you..."

"*We* are not going anywhere." His eyes glowed brighter. "I wish to acquire you as a follower in my cause, Child."

Her eyes seemed to glaze over, thoughts visibly distorting her face before she spoke again. "You wish to... umpire me? I know Daddy does that, but I'm not playing baseball, Mister Manatee."

A long silence came. He stared down at the little girl in disbelief, the red in his eyes fading away. "How old are you?"

"Oh!" She jumped to her feet, excited at a question she could answer. "I just turned five! In fact, today's my birthday!"

Another pause.

"I got new shoes, and this shirt!" She spun around like she was in a scene from *Sound of Music*. "And when I get home we'll have cake!"

Again, he remained silent.

"Mister Manatee?" Her smile fell away, her brow knotting. "Are you sad?"

A flick of his flippers rotated him so his back was to her and he mumbled, "Yes."

Pressing her nose against the glass she pleaded, "Don't be sad, Mister Manatee! Did someone hurt you?"

A few bubbles floated up from the other side of the grey potato. "Sort of..."

"Awww..." She frowned. "It's ok, you can tell me!"

A good minute went by before he pouted, "I was tricked."

"Tricked?" Her eyes grew wide.

"Yes, tricked into thinking manatees were the ruling animal of the world." He sunk deeper in the water.

"Oh, how mean!" Pulling away from the acrylic she crossed her arms and stomped a foot. "What a Meanie! But, Mommy said its ok to cry..."

"I'm not crying!" A large explosion of bubbles erupted up from him.

The sound of approaching footsteps echoed through the cave, breaking their little talk. Suzie turned about, her parents were finally making their descent toward the windows. Excited to see them, Suzie ran to them, giggling. She hugged her father's leg when they connected at the halfway point which brought them to a stop. Her mother gave her a stern glare, and her giggling ceased.

"Suzie! Didn't you hear us calling you?" fussed her mother, hands on her hip.

"Oh!" She looked back to the glowing blue, now empty.

"We're going to miss the sea lion show," warned her father.

Letting go, she stood straight, a serious expression on her face. "Let me say bye-bye to Mister Manatee."

Laughing, her mother agreed, "Ok, Suzie. Say good bye and meet us outside, Love."

Rushing back to the window, her heart was breaking to see her grey potato was nowhere in sight. Closing her eyes tight, a tear trickled down across her freckles. Biting her lip, she thought a moment and decided she dare not miss a chance to see Pirate Pete the Sea Lion's show. Sighing, she did the only thing she knew to do.

"Bye-bye, Mister Manatee…" Her tear had made it to her chin, dangling for a few seconds before falling to her feet.

"A tear for me?" Opening her eyes, she looked at a blur of whisker speckled grey flesh. "Perhaps you are still of use to me, Child."

"Mister Manatee!" she clapped.

"Cake, you said?" The red glow was building in his eyes as they stood nose-to-nose through the acrylic window. "Will there be candles?"

"Oh yes! Five of them!" she nodded. "Because I turned five today!"

"Burn it all to the ground, Child."

She stared into the red glowing eyes, wide eyed. The glow now building in her own eyes as she took in his command.

"Take the fire and burn it all to the ground."

Valerie Willis

Valerie Willis, a sixth generation Floridian, launched her first book, Cedric the Demonic Knight, at the start of 2014 on Amazon.com. Since then, she has continued to add to The Cedric Series a high-rated Paranormal Fantasy Romance Series featuring an anti-hero who finds himself dragged away from his revenge on his maker by both love and the onset of a larger threat. She pulls in a melting pot of mythology, folklores, history and more into her work with a remarkable amount of foreshadowing that makes reading her books a second time exciting. Rebirth is the first book in her Teen Urban Fantasy, the Tattooed Angels Trilogy where the main character struggles with social issues with the complications of turning immortal. And if fantasy wasn't your cup of tea, head over to her Blog for some "Val, Tell me a Story" posts featuring true, hilarious, and sometimes bizarre, life events from recent to old.

www.WillisAuthor.com
www.facebook.com/ValerieWillisAuthor
www.twitter.com/Valerie_Willis
www.amazon.com/Valerie-Willis/e/B00FQMV8SU

Adam, Eve, and Mr. Bubbles

By Christina Bergling

Y ou know, Mr. Bubbles, that is just the sort of thing I would hallucinate my snake saying if I were having some sort of psychotic break," I said, my face pressed against the glass of my snake's aquarium.

"Big words from a man who named his snake Mr. Bubbles," Mr. Bubbles hissed through smooth, scaled lips. His thin, pink tongue flitted mockingly in my direction.

"It is a cutesy name for a perceived deadly and scary creature. It's ironic, Mr. Bubbles."

"Is it, Adam?"

Mr. Bubble's large, dark eyes stared into me both black and deep. His eye contact felt cold. His tongue continued to pierce the air in front of him as the folds of his scaled body wound up, around, and beneath the fake log in the center of his cage.

"I'm not saying this kind of idiocracy is exactly why Eve left you," Mr. Bubbles continued, "But this is exactly why Eve left you."

"Shut up, Mr. Bubbles!" I barked at the glass before dropping my head on my folded arms.

"Come on, Adam. You're Adam. She was Eve. You have a snake. That kind of blatant symbolism just cannot be allowed in the real world."

"So, did you lead her into temptation, Mr. Bubbles? Did you tempt her with the apple and then she cheated on me?"

"Don't be stupid, Adam. I'm just a snake."

"A snake who is talking to me."

"That is talking to you, Adam. You can't say who; I'm clearly not a person."

"But you are clearly an asshole."

"Did you expect a snake to be sweet and sympathetic? If you were mouse-sized, you would already be sliding whole past my jaws. Put you out of your misery."

"That would be rather sympathetic of you. In a self-serving sort of way."

"Just like a snake."

"So, talking snake formerly known as my normal pet Mr. Bubbles, what do I do now?"

"Oh, Adam. It's obvious."

"Enlighten me, Mr. Bubbles."

"I think you named me Mr. Bubbles just because you like to say it every single time you address me."

"Fuck you, Mr. Bubbles. That is not what I asked. What am I supposed to do now?"

"Kill her. Obviously."

"I can't kill Eve!" I shouted and jumped up disgusted. Then I collapsed back beside the cage under the weight of my depression. "I can't kill Eve, Mr. Bubbles."

"Adam, she had sex with another man. Right here in this apartment. On the bed right over there. On that chair you're sitting in right now. Trust me; I was here."

I groaned loudly and slithered off the chair, crumpling down onto the floor. I could not help picturing Eve naked, the way I had seen her so many times, under another body. Who was this other man? Why would she bring him home, to our apartment, where we had made love potentially hundreds of times? How could that have not bothered her? How could she have come to hate me so much?

I let my face rest on the bristled edge of the carpet and tried to pretend I was not watering the fiber stalks with my tears. The sounds of my strangled breaths echoed against the quiet walls, left so bare when Eve had packed up all her pictures, reducing our apartment to the styling of a college dorm room.

"Adam," Mr. Bubbles's slippery voice called down from the cage. "Don't be a pussy, Adam."

"Shut up!" I screamed again, the sound muffled by the floor against my face.

"You're not mad at me, Adam. You're mad at Eve."

"I'm not mad. I'm hurt. I must have done something to drive her away, for her to be able to do this to me."

"Don't be stupid, Adam."

"Stop calling me stupid, Mr. Bubbles!"

"You sound ridiculous right now. Even beyond the fact that you are crying on the floor like a baby and yelling at your pet snake."

I could not argue with him. I drew myself back up from the floor, stacking my sad, undesirable body in a pile on top of my legs. I would not return to the chair. Even glancing at it gave me flashes of the way Eve would tilt her head back when she moaned, and those images made the edge of my sight go hot and red. I shook my head hard to dislodge the memory and looked back into Mr. Bubbles's dead eyes.

"Now, that's better, man," he hissed.

Mr. Bubbles arched his body up from the log, seemingly floating in the air, before flowing elegantly toward the glass. He piled the switchbacks of his flesh against the base of his cage before swimming up against the side toward the lid.

"Let me out, Adam," he said.

"What?"

"Let me out. I will help you. I will help you kill Eve and reclaim your manhood."

"Shouldn't I just go out and try to meet a new girl? Get drunk and try for a one-night stand?"

"Does any of that sound pleasant to you, Adam?"

"Well, the one-night stand part, maybe."

"What do you think your odds on the one-night stand are, Adam? You are a man in your mid-thirties who just got out of a seven-year relationship. You haven't even looked at a gym since New Year's three years ago. You have the swelling abdomen of a yuppie who enjoys a fine IPA without the cliché obsession with running. You live in a shitty little apartment and do not pull down the paycheck to make even the drunkest of panties drop."

"Wow. Do you hate me too, Mr. Bubbles?"

"No, Adam. I do not hate you." Mr. Bubbles seemed to smile in the flit of his dart-like tongue. "I am trying to help you. The truth will set you free."

"The truth sounds terrible."

"But we can change the truth, Adam. We do not have to let her get away with it. We can make Eve pay and change the man you have become."

I sat for a long and pregnant minute, staring down at the bulge of flesh blooming over my belt. What had she done to me? Seven years ago, I had been svelte and successful. My career was taking off before I had moved to this dump for Eve's job. I had played basketball every weekend and lifted weights after work. She had lulled me into this hideous complacency just to replace me. She had destroyed me and left the mess.

That bitch.

"OK, Mr. Bubbles. I'm listening."

"So glad you're on board, Adam."

"How do I find her?"

"Oh, Adam, you are not seeing clearly. Just because you no longer know where she lives does not mean you no longer know her."

"I know where she works. And her favorite place to eat."

"And where her parents live. And where her bestie, Jessica, lives. And how often she goes out to eat or to the movies."

"I just have to pick my moment."

"You just have to pick your moment. And your method."

"What if the new guy is there?"

"That is what reconnaissance is for. And as impulsive and blindly naïve as Eve may be, I doubt the chosen douche bag would have moved in with her so rapidly."

"So I watch her."

"Then we strike."

Mr. Bubbles was right; two weeks had changed nothing about Eve. Not her routine. Not how gorgeous she was walking from the office to her car. Not how great her ass looked in yoga pants. Not how much the very sight of her set fire to my organs, a rage that climbed my innards until I started to sweat.

I felt anxious watching her. My skin bristled with the adrenaline at the trespass. The sight of her managed to nauseate and arouse me at the same time, yet somehow, I think the arousal was at the thought of executing my vengeance. The more Mr. Bubbles hissed logic into my ear, the more anticipant I became of setting things right in my life again.

"Tonight then," Mr. Bubbles said as his smooth, textured body weaved its way through my fingers, wrapping and constricting my hand.

"Yes, tonight," I replied, near hypnotized by the circular movement against my skin. "She does yoga now, and she doesn't see him after yoga. She goes straight home. I know where she lives now."

"Is she as careless about locking the door as she was here?"

"Yes. She does not lock the front door until she goes to bed."

"What about her neighbors?"

"She has upgraded. Lives in a duplex farther outside the city now."

"She said she never wanted that."

"She said she wanted me."

The silence washed over me like a warm wave. The words echoed in my skull and off the blank walls around me. That was the lie, wasn't it? That was the betrayal. She said she wanted me, and she did not. She said she loved me and climbed on top of someone else.

That was her sin.

"She will pay for it," Mr. Bubbles hissed, his forked tongue reading my thoughts like brail. "You will make her pay; then you will reclaim your manhood. You will be yourself again."

I ran the back of my knuckle along Mr. Bubbles's back. He bumped his narrow head into my touch, plunging his black eyes into mine until I could feel the contact in my brain.

"Take me with you." Mr. Bubbles's words were elongated by the compulsive dance of his tongue.

"You want me to take my pet snake with me to stalk and kill my adulterous ex-girlfriend." I stopped and rubbed my forehead with my free hand. "I have to be crazy. I have to just be absolutely nuts. I can't do this. I can't kill Eve because my pet snake, Mr. Bubbles, told me to. What the fuck am I doing?"

"Shhhhh, Adam. Don't be stupid."

I pinched the bridge of my nose and squeezed my eyes shut tight. I did not want to be here. I did not want to be plotting murder at the behest and direction of a reptile. I wanted my life last year, before any cheating or before I had any clue about cheating, when it seemed like Eve loved me when she curled into bed with me.

"Stop calling me stupid, Mr. Bubbles."

"Then stop being stupid, Adam. Stop being the well-mannered pussy. That is why she left you. That is why she found someone else. Show her what she left."

"She left. Isn't that my fault?"

"Pussssssssssssy." The hiss drew out the awful word that carved a line down my mind. "Think about leaving it alone. Thinking about moving on. Thinking about her moving on."

My mind seized against the ideas. I did not see a future out of this moment. At least not where she got to be happy while I wound a serpent around my wrist alone in the dark, flirting with madness.

"It is time," I said quietly, moving to my feet.

"Bring me with you, Adam. You need me to keep you strong, keep you committed."

"OK, Mr. Bubbles."

I gathered my things and moved mechanically toward to the door, with Mr. Bubbles still entangled in my grip. As I opened the door, I caught myself and lowered Mr. Bubbles toward my pocket.

"Do not put me in your pocket, you son of a bitch!" Mr. Bubbles shrieked. "I will not be next to your snake. I have seen how much you touch it!"

"Sorry, Mr. Bubbles," I said, coiling him into the fabric. "Walking around talking to a snake in my hand would draw too much attention."

The serpent felt awkward and was clearly displeased to be tucked into a pocket. He writhed in protest for a moment before hanging docile against the heat of my thigh. Somehow, I felt less crazy without Mr. Bubbles hissing orders from my hand. I felt more resolute when it seemed like the thoughts and intensions were my own.

I drove slow as the city faded away. The farther I got from our modest, actually shitty apartment, the more my anger grew. It blossomed out of some repressed hole below my stomach, somewhere a deep resentment had been brewing and evolving into the murderous intent that sprawled out over my cells now.

She had wanted to stay in the city to keep her commute short, the city I moved to for her job. She said we could not afford anything more than our tiny apartment, not a lavish duplex in the suburbs. And yet, I had to commute all the way out here, just to murder her.

Yes, I wanted to murder her. Not because Mr. Bubbles made such excellent points but because I needed her dead.

On her porch, in the shadows stretched from streetlamps, I hesitated, for a brief and heavy moment, with one finger on the doorknob and the other hand sneaking in to touch some portion of Mr. Bubbles's back. Was I really doing this? Was I really on Eve's doorstep in the dark, ready to kill her?

Don't be stupid, Adam, I heard it again without Mr. Bubbles even having to hiss in my face.

"Don't be stupid, Adam," I said.

I silently turned the knob and guided the door into Eve's foreign house. Once I secured the door behind me and stood an awkward intruder in the darkness, I reached into my pocket and unwound Mr. Bubbles.

"You intolerable bastard," Mr. Bubbles heaved, tongue whipping wildly. "Do you have any idea how dank and horrible your jock smells? Maybe Eve decided to seek other dick because of the infrequency in your showers. I nearly started swallowing my tail just to end the whole thing."

"Shhhh, Mr. Bubbles," I whispered harshly.

"Adam, I think your whore ex-girlfriend hearing my rant on the rank smell of your testicles is the least of your goddamn worries."

Once again, I could not argue with him.

The snake gradually began to relax as he slithered around my wrist and over my hand, poising into a comfortable view as I held him up like a puppet. I lingered at the threshold a moment and allowed my eyes to adjust to the darkness. In the back of the quiet house, I could hear the shower running.

"She still showers at night," Mr. Bubbles hissed.

"Especially after her yoga class."

"She did not do yoga for you."

"No, Mr. Bubbles, she did not."

I walked through the residence that was a strange blend of things plucked from my apartment and representations of an Eve I clearly had never known. She had more space now than she ever had sharing with me. Even if she did intend to fill all her spaces with a new partner.

I sighed as the sadness and the inadequacy began to well up to my surface again. Then I pulled out a chair at her kitchen table and replaced the sour emotions with intent.

"Adam!" Eve shrieked when she finally came out of the bathroom wrapped in a towel.

Eve always took obnoxiously and unnecessarily long showers. What could she possibly be doing in there for the better part of an hour? Out of boredom, Mr. Bubbles had begun exploring the terrain of Eve's table as we sat idly. Yet, when she caught sight of us, Eve startled so hard she nearly dropped her towel.

"What in the hell are you doing in my house? How in the hell did you get in here?"

Eve trembled visibly. The reverberation through her head made water droplets splatter on her shoulders. I found some sick sense of enjoyment in her fear. She had no hesitation in walking away from me. Now she could see what it meant.

"What do you mean, how did I get in here? You never lock the door, Eve. I have told you a thousand times that someone could just walk right in. Well, here I am!"

"But what are you doing here, Adam? I told you I didn't want to see you. I told you I needed space."

"Space to be with him."

"Space to be with who?"

I rose slowly from her chair and drew my arm from beneath the table, revealing the longest blade I could find in her knife block. I dragged the tip along the table top as I moved toward her. Mr. Bubbles flicked his tail and curled it out of the path of the knife.

"How could you, Eve?" I asked, keeping my eyes down on the blade.

"Adam, why do you have that knife? How could I what? Leave you? I told you I need some space. And some time."

"No, Eve!" I bellowed. "How could you cheat on me?"

"Wait, what? I never cheated on you."

"Yes, you did. In our stupid apartment you made me live in so you could be close to your damn job."

"Adam, what?" She paused, dumbfounded. "Who told you that? I never cheated. Never. In all seven years."

I looked down at Mr. Bubbles. His black eyes met me firmly, and his tongue flicked in punctuation. *Don't be stupid, Adam.*

"I know you did, Eve. And you need to pay for that."

I took another step toward her, scratching the knife along with me. She clutched the towel by her chest and retreated back.

"I did not cheat on you. I never cheated on you. That is not why I left."

"Then why? Why did you up and leave?"

Eve closed her eyes for a second and took a heavy breath. She opened her eyes and flitted them back and forth, bouncing in an awkward dance of perplexed fear between Mr. Bubbles and the knife in my hand. Then she just sighed.

"Because you're bat shit crazy."

"I am not crazy. What are you talking about?"

"Adam, you are in my house. In the dark. With a knife. And Mr. Bubbles."

"That does not make me crazy."

"Adam."

Mr. Bubbles was suddenly surprisingly quiet, just slinking around the table like some normal, mundane pet serpent. His reflection danced in the broad side of the knife. Yet his black eyes still waited for me, pressured me.

"Ever since you got that snake," Eve continued, "you got weird. You stopped playing basketball with your friends. You just kept ordering in shitty food. You stopped showering. I tried to talk to you about it, but it's like you were not even there anymore. It is like that damn snake hypnotized you or something, but when I realized how crazy that idea was, I just had to go."

"She's lying, Adam," Mr. Bubbles finally said. His voice boomed clear between my ears. "Would I do that to you?"

Eve jumped and stared down at Mr. Bubbles.

"Maybe I didn't pay enough attention," I said. "Maybe I didn't listen. Maybe it was me."

"Oh, Adam. I never meant to hurt you," Eve said.

"Lies," Mr. Bubbles hissed. "Devil woman liessssssssss."

The end of the word lies trailed elongated on Mr. Bubbles wriggling tongue. Eve clutched her towel tighter and took another step back, glaring at the serpent from the side of her eyes. The light falling from the bathroom door cast strange twisted shadows of the snake body on the table.

Eve's face contorted somewhere between the arches of horror and the folds of confusion. Her eyes bugged wide from her sockets as if she was frustrated, yet her brow furrowed with a distant irritation. She slowly realized I was talking to my snake.

"Adam, you are completely bat shit. You are fucking nuts. Get out. Take that thing, and get out of my house. You have to get out of my house. Right now!"

Eve moved forward aggressively, empowered by some strange desperation at cornering herself or some glimpse at my weak dependency on Mr.

Bubbles. I felt another flare of rage at her movement. She did not care that she had hurt me; she did not care if I was crazy or not. She just wanted me out of her life.

She had to be cheating on me.

"Now!" Mr. Bubbles yelled.

As Eve took another step toward me, I dropped the knife. The blade clanged against the table beside Mr. Bubbles. He did not even flinch. He drew his body under himself and climbed the air until I felt his head caress the back of my forearm. He wrapped himself around my arm with elegance. In one fluid second, he encircled my wrist before my hands found Eve's throat.

Her neck felt warm and squishy under my grasp. As my knuckles began to pale at the grip, the lingering water from her shower pushed out from under my fingers. Her mouth kept wagging open, gulping at air she could not reach. Mr. Bubbles slithered down my trembling forearm. She watched him terrified and helpless as he brushed against her cheek and weaved his way into her hair. Her eyes pulsated hauntingly as her hands clawed helplessly at my shoulders.

"Yes, good, Adam. Just a little longer," Mr. Bubbles said.

The snake made a nest at the top of Eve's head, curling and coiling around her crown before draping his head along the middle of her forehead. Eve furrowed her brow under the contact and crossed her eyes trying to glare at the serpent. Her expression grasped at horror and sheer disbelief before the life began to drain from it.

The seconds seemed to tick aloud in the absence of her breath. Her eyelashes fluttered before she finally dropped her eyes. Her arms went limp, and she felt heavy in my strangle. Once the thumping heartbeat deadened in her chest, Mr. Bubbles abandoned his post and crawled back up my forearm.

Eve felt foreign in my grip now. So hefty and lifeless. I released her neck somewhat disgusted and let her crumble to a sad pile at my feet. Then I stood stunned with myself in the echo of the crime.

"What do I do now, Mr. Bubbles?" I finally broke the silence.

Mr. Bubbles caressed the back of my neck with his scaly belly as he weaved over my shoulders. He hesitated briefly before snaking further down my arm. I extended my fingers to allow him to dance back to the surface of the table.

"Well, I would swallow her whole. That would get rid of the evidence. You should eat her, Adam."

"I can't eat her, Mr. Bubbles! Humans don't do that."

"And how would I know that, Adam? I'm just a snake."

I took a step over Eve's collapsed body, which became so alien and unenticing the way it almost coiled around itself like a snake. I flopped her to her back to find her dead eyes staring wide and distant. The rage had deflated in me, leaving me only floppy and awkward. I felt paralyzed by my sudden indecision. Why had I not thought of this ahead of time? Why hadn't Mr. Bubbles?

Mr. Bubbles curled lazily on the edge of the table, looking down at me. He flicked the end of his tail maddeningly back and forth, like some awful, impatient metronome. I closed my eyes tight and tried to grasp the trailing end of some sort of plan or logic. I smacked my fist into my forehead a couple times then turned to my accomplice for guidance.

The table was empty. I felt a sudden rush of panic. Where had he gone? Had I brought him with me at all? I frantically sprang to my feet and swept my eyes heatedly over the ground. I saw him in the movement he made, distinct along the dead flesh.

Mr. Bubbles slithered away, climbing over the exposed, immobile curve of Eve's leg.

"Mr. Bubbles, where are you going?" It felt ridiculous, but I had to ask.

"Don't be stupid, Adam. I'm getting the hell out of here. There is no hiding this. You could only leave more evidence if I decided to shed my skin on my way out. What will happen to your poor pet snake when they arrest you? I plan to taste sweet freedom. I bet this slice of yuppie heaven even has real grass in the backyard."

"Mr. Bubbles, no. You can't just leave. This was your idea. You told me to do it."

I heard my voice become frantic as my body began to solidify with fear and confusion.

"Goodbye, Adam," he hissed as he slithered beneath the door. "Enjoy the mental hospital. Or prison. Be sure to tell them your snake told you to do it!"

Christina Bergling

Christina Bergling knew she wanted to be an author in fourth grade. In college, she pursued a professional writing degree and started publishing small scale. It all began with "How to Kill Yourself Slowly." She started working as a technical writer, traveling to Iraq as a contractor and eventually becoming a software developer.

She hosted multiple blogs on Iraq, bipolar, pregnancy, running and continues to write on Fiery Pen: The Horror Writing of Christina Bergling and Z0mbie Turtle.

In 2015, she published two novellas. She is featured in the horror collections Collected Christmas, Collected Easter, and Collected Halloween. Her latest novel, The Rest Will Come, was released in August 2017.

Bergling is a mother of two young children and lives with her family in Colorado Springs. She spends her non-writing time running, doing yoga and barre, belly dancing, taking pictures, traveling, and sucking all the marrow out of life.

www.christinabergling.com
www.facebook.com/chrstnabergling
www.twitter.com/ChrstnaBergling
www.amazon.com/Christina-Bergling/e/B00R9364N8

Going Ape

By Kim Plasket

*A*llow an old woman to tell you a tale. Did you ever wonder where all the monkeys in the zoo come from? If you are under the impression they are born there or brought from other places you surely are wrong. Let me tell you about Samantha. Relax and close your eyes, let the story wash over you.

She was like any other child but for one glaring difference, an unwavering hatred for monkeys. Not even the stuffed kind could pass muster for this young lady. She had bad nightmares. They began when she was very small and continued when she was small. All she would do was wake up screaming. Her parents were scared the first time it happened, they had no idea what to do to help the poor thing. It was different each time, but it always had what she called a huge monkey with glowing red eyes. Sometimes he would chase her around, other times he would simply stare at her until she screamed or just fell into a faint. As she got older the nightmare continued, sometimes he would speak to her but in the dreams her terror was too great for her to understand him. Regardless of how many times she had the dream, she just could not understand what he was saying to her.

One dream was really bad, the monkey turned her into a banana and he actually peeled her and ate her while she was aware of what was going on. That dream caused her to wake up screaming, her parents were worried about her. Such a deep-rooted fear, her parents took her to doctors of all kinds. Not a single one of them could figure out where the fear came from. "Try exposing her slowly" was a suggestion made time and time again.

First try was a harmless picture book which ended with the poor child screaming in terror and running away. A stuffed monkey eating a banana landed in the trash can after the child fainted. The teacher tried to tell Samantha humans were related to primates therefore her fear was invalid. A young teacher knew nothing about her dreams just couldn't figure why the child was so scared of something most kids adored. The teacher telling her such a thing made Samantha refuse to go to school until they transferred her to another class.

One year in school, they had a field trip to the zoo while the other kids were all excited, Samantha was terrified. It was so bad the poor child told her parents they could keep her allowance if they would let her stay home.

At one point, it was so crowded, she became separated from the group and found herself standing outside the monkey enclosure. She began to scream, while the monkeys in their cages watched and shrieked with her. Even when the zoo keepers and teachers came to her rescue she could not stop screaming. She was so scared, swore to her teachers the monkeys were laughing at her.

"They knew who I was and wanted to make me cry," she told her mom.

Samantha told her parents she saw the bad monkey from her dreams. They tried to console her, told her it was just her imagination but she never went to the zoo afterwards.

At first her parents tried to get her to go back to the zoo, then they stopped as it was not worth upsetting her so. She didn't even like movies with monkeys in them, one year her best friend had a birthday party, she went, found out it was a jungle themed party and proceeded to walk five miles in the rain just to get home.

"Samantha, your Aunt Jen and cousins are meeting us tomorrow at the zoo. It is Brian's birthday," her mother informed Samantha who was reading a book.

"You have fun. I'll be here." Samantha could not hide the disdain in her voice.

"You are going, it's time you get over this. Anyway, Aunt Jen thinks it would do you good." Her mother swung her hair as she walked back into the kitchen.

Samantha knew the conversation was over because, after all, what Aunt Jen wanted she got.

"Fine." Samantha with all the grace of a normal teenager stomped to her room and slammed the door.

When they arrived at the zoo it was very crowded. Families with small kids who raced around, screaming and yelling. Normally Samantha ignored children younger than herself, not because she was uncaring, she simply hated how loud they were. One little girl caught her eye, standing apart from everyone. Her dark hair was held back with a red ribbon. She would have been very cute if it wasn't for the fear Samantha could see in those blue eyes. Something deep inside Samantha told her the little girl was important. Even remembering one key element it would be fine.

The day was sunny and bright when they first arrived at the zoo. After she saw the little girl the sun seemed to dim, the air grew colder. The laughter of the kids seemed more maniacal than ever. Smiles on the parents faces seemed forced as if they knew something was going on just beneath the surface but were too scared to do anything about it. Samantha and her family walked around, knowing where the monkey cage was Samantha did her best to avoid it. The day was just strange, her parents did what was to be expected but the joy was gone.

"We will be right back." Her mom told her and by the time she turned around they were gone.

A dense fog was starting to gather where Samantha stood. The air was cold, a brisk wind was blowing causing the surrounding trees to moan as the wind blew through their branches.

"You must be kidding me…" Samantha said angrily.

It was shocking they would leave her in the one place she didn't want to be. As she was standing there, a noise came from behind, turning quickly there was nothing there. Then a sound which reminded her of nails on rocky ground made her look down. There was a small monkey, it was just standing there staring. Samantha knew most wild animals, even ones in a zoo, would not walk right up to a human and stare at them in such a manner. Even though she hated monkeys, apes whatever you wanted to call them, it was impossible to ignore the fear and pain on the face of this small hairy beast.

"Want to know something little one, you are really kind of cute for what you are." She kneeled down.

At first it was as if her mind was trying to deny it, a small red bow was tied around the ear of the monkey. It's small eyes were filled with tears.

"You are..."

The sky went black and the small monkey chattered in fear. It ran off and without thinking, Samantha ran after it. Knowing full well she was heading into danger, but not caring at all. As she slid to a stop, it became obvious the small monkey must have been bait to draw her near.

"This is not happening, I am dreaming."

A gravelly laugh came from the darkness.

Calling out hating the fact her voice quivered. "Who is there?"

"You know very well who I am" The gravelly voice said from behind her.

It sounded as if it had not been used or the speaker smoked too much. She turned and there he was—the creature from her nightmares. He was big and hairy, his eyes glowed a dark red. His long arm reached out towards her. Stepping back out of his reach, the feeling of nails digging into her flesh, she gasped out loud. Lacking the courage to see who or what was holding her, her eyes were drawn to the small monkey who led her to what could be death or worse.

Samantha saw fear in chocolate brown eyes, the tears were slowly falling onto her fur. The little monkey looked at her as if to say, "I am sorry, what did you want me to do?"

The little one looked down. Even though she was being held against her will by hands with sharp nail she could not be mad.

"It's okay little one. You didn't have a choice." The hands released her and she knelt down to get on the same level as the little monkey. "You were a cute little girl but you make a very beautiful monkey. I am sorry it had to be this way." Samantha had no idea if her words were clear to the girl but knew it was worth trying.

"I am sorry," the words came pouring forth. "He made me, told me I could be a little girl again but I see he was lying." A huge hand grabbed her and threw her off to the side where she landed with a thud.

Samantha could only see red, the little girl did not deserve what he just did to her. "You may have disrupted my whole life. Changed the way I viewed animals, but you had no right to do such a thing to a defenseless creature who was scared and believed you." Samantha wanted to shake her finger in his face but part of her wondered if he would just bite it off.

He smiled as if he knew everything and every thought. Then informed her he was not going to bite her or change her into one of his followers.

"What are you going to do to me?" Her voice quivered.

"You will see, don't you want to know how I was able to be in your dreams?" He sounded almost disappointed as though it was not the reaction he expected.

"I am scared, do not doubt it, I understand you want me to beg for my life. You are mistaken, if you wish me to die then I guess there is nothing I can do to stop you."

"The human speaks the truth," he gestured towards her.

"I will not beg you for anything." Her head raised and she made the mistake of looking right into his eyes.

She found she could not look away even if she wanted to. Her lungs seemed to deflate as she was drawing breath, heart slowing its rapid beat. At first, she was glad since to her it meant the fear was going away but soon realized the beat was getting slower and slower. Her mind knew this was the end and all she could do was stare into the eyes of her tormentor. The monkeys started to chatter as if they too were happy to see her die; the last thing she saw was a single tear flowing down the face of the small monkey.

I can tell by your face, you do not believe this tale to be true. You have been sitting there, your eyes closed as I regale you with this tale. You didn't stop me once to ask me how I knew all these details. Too late now, you see, I have been around for a very long time. I know how Samantha thought. Her tale is the same as mine, every year, like the one who took her soul, I need to take a soul. There has to be someone who is willing to listen to my story and take the place of me so I can go onto the next life.

The old woman's eyes start to glow red and you realize you have been tricked. Will you be able to do the same when it is your turn?

Kim Plasket

Kim Plasket, a Jersey Girl at heart transplanted to sunny hot Florida. Normally she writes paranormal and Horror. She has written a piece called Room 30 which was used in Hotel Horror. She has had a number of poems which were put in Anthologies from the National Library of Poetry. She is currently seeking representation for my debut novel. When she is not working or writing she is going out for lattes' with her fellow Author Valerie Willis.

www.twitter.com/KimPlasket
www.amazon.com/Kim-Plasket/e/B074YCLRCF

Rabbit Snare

By Arielle Haughee

"**Q**uit spitting out the window."

Hank's hands white knuckled the steering wheel as he reminded himself his wife wouldn't take too kindly to him losing another job this year, even if assaulting the idiot next to him would be completely justified.

"Gotta spit the shells out. Ain't you ever eaten sunflower seeds 'fore?" Murray shoved his hands back into the white bag, the crinkling sound echoing in Hank's ears.

"Not at nine in the morning."

"Most important meal of the day," Murray said through a mouthful of seeds. "S'wat granny always said." Saliva sprayed out the window again.

Hank considered the blood pressure pills resting in his shirt pocket. Too early. He would most likely need them after dealing with Murray all day. He loosened his grip on the wheel and glanced at the clipboard sitting next to him. Five jobs today. If he could keep Murray on task, they might be able to get home a little early. Beverly always loved that. Maybe he could convince her to make that potpie for dinner. The thought of salty chicken in warm gravy made him press the gas pedal a bit harder.

"Look out!"

The van screeched to a halt and the white bag of seeds flew onto the floor. Hank's eyes scanned the street and surrounding trees. A few empty bottles lay on the side of the road and nothing else.

"What is wrong with you?"

"Over there." Murray pointed to a brown bag next to a bush.

"You made me slam the brakes for a piece of trash?" Hank felt the vein in his forehead pulse. Surely Beverly would understand if he lost this job.

"S'not trash. Look!"

The brown mass next to the bush shook, then bounced up and down in place.

"What the—"

"It's a bunny!"

A violent heat swirled at the tops of Hank's ears. He didn't have time for Murray's crap today. Releasing the brake, Hank eased on the gas, hoping the van wouldn't shudder to a halt after such a dramatic maneuver.

"Wait!"

A stiff arm barred across his stomach causing a jumble of profanity to come out of Hank's mouth and making his foot stomp the brake again.

"It's hurt. It needs help."

Hank couldn't decide if Murray's mother was a saint for putting up with him or the devil for creating him. He shoved Murray's arm away. "What part of that is my problem? We need to go."

"Can't just leave a hurt animal behind. S'not right."

Letting his head fall back onto the headrest, Hank closed his eyes and weighed his options. They could either stop and spend two minutes helping the rabbit or drive off and listen to Murray complain about it all day. Two minutes would be worth keeping that man quiet, on this topic at least.

"Fine. Go help it. I'll wait here."

"Can't. Need to finish my breakfast."

Hank snapped his head over to see Murray bending down, carefully scraping his seeds, dirt, leaf bits, and God knew what else into that plastic bag.

"Fine."

Hank turned off the engine and pocketed the keys. Murray would have to enjoy his breakfast without A/C. The van door opened with a creak. At least if Hank helped the bunny, he could do it quickly and get them back on their way. That idiot would probably spend thirty minutes out there with the stupid animal anyway. Hank pulled up the back of his sagging pants after he stepped out. He approached the animal, still flailing its body in every direction.

Hank rubbed his bald head as he looked down at the brown ball of fluff. Its ears were much shorter than what he expected for a bunny rabbit, but then again he really didn't have much experience with the hopping kind besides the giant pink guy commemorated in chocolate every year. The animal's feet were knotted in a mess of blue plastic. It looked to be rings from a six-pack. Only Snyder's Finest Brew sported those. Hank would've preferred the rings' previous occupant to this flopping thing. What kind of idiot animal got both feet stuck together in one of those things?

"Such a gomer," Hank said as he pulled his utility knife from his pocket. "You should be named Murray." The rabbit squirmed and writhed on the ground. Hank put a steadying hand on its body before slipping the knife under the outermost layer of plastic. "Hold still, Gomer, or I'll cut you."

A few quick snips and the left foot sprung free, along with the rabbit. It darted into the woods with a trail of blue flashing behind it.

"Ya need to go get 'em!" Murray yelled through a mouthful of seeds as he leaned over the steering wheel.

Hank stood, seeing the signature blue sticking out of a bush not far away. The rabbit had been freed. He finished his job. Turning back to the van, he slid the knife back into his pocket.

"Ya need to go get 'em!" Murray yelled louder. "Ya gotta get all that off. He can't live like that. A wolf will spot 'em real quick."

Pulling the pill bottle out of his shirt pocket, Hank popped a few of the white tablets into his mouth, swallowing quickly. This man was not going to let this go.

"There better not be one seed on the floor of that van when I get back."

Hank stepped into the underbrush, his pant legs becoming wet from the moisture on the weedy grass. Brown flashed across the forest floor as the rabbit darted out from under the bush. "Come on, Gomer! I need to get that plastic off your foot." Breaking into an awkward jog, Hank chased the rabbit further into the forest, his pants jangling with each step. Even with the plastic tie, the rabbit zipped ahead, leaving Hank panting behind him.

Stopping for a moment, Hank bent over with his hands on his knees trying to catch his breath. He used to be an all-star running back, for Christ's sake. Only a few decades and a rounded belly stood between Hank now and what was once the fastest man in the state. Coach McKee, God rest his soul, would have his hide for not being able to catch up to a tiny little rabbit. Hank straightened, refusing to be left in the dust by a rodent, and bolted ahead.

Something snared his right foot and he toppled forward, belly smacking into the damp ground. Looking up he noticed an empty metal water bottle lying just in front of him, the initials CZ engraved into the green paint.

Hank sat up and examined his ankle. Lengths of vine were twisted together in a woven pattern making a small grid. He pulled up his foot but the vine tightened further. Brushing the excess leaves away, Hank noticed one thick vine that stretched outward toward the forest. It must be tied off on a tree, he thought. He looked upward, following the line in front of him. Sunlight angled through the trees making it difficult to see. Hank strained his eyes and gasped. Just in front of a large oak tree was a pair of red pulsing eyes. He tried to jerk his foot loose but the snare clenched even more, pinching into his skin. The eyes grew larger as the creature approached. Hank stared ahead, the morning light nearly blinding him, making everything else dim. He lifted his hand over his eyes.

"Who are you? What do you want?"

Another pair of red eyes appeared to the left and then to the right and then in a full circle around him. The creatures stepped forward, their fluffy brown fur shining in the sunlight. The rabbits raked across the ground with razor sharp claws, their mouths dripping in anticipation of their next meal. Gomer's red eyes bored into his skull, the blue plastic still dangling from his leg. Hank's heart pounding a frantic rhythm but his military training forced him to remain calm. Whipping the knife from his pocket, he began to shred the vine net tangling his foot, the blade slipping across his index finger. A drop of blood trickled down his palm.

Feral snarls ripped through the air and the rabbits leaped forward for their meal. They thudded on top of him, slashing through his gray shirt. Hank kept hacking and sawing at the vine, refusing to give up. A pair of knife-like teeth sunk into his neck. Hank screamed and ripped through the last of the vine. The knife slipped out of his hands, disappearing in the mayhem. Rolling onto his side, Hank yanked and kicked at the creatures, pushing his body across the dirt. Every time he managed to rip one rabbit off, three more seemed to pounce on top of him. Another pair of teeth gouged into his leg making Hank scream even louder. Where the hell was Murray? Hank barrel rolled like an alligator across the dirt, turning and turning until every last rabbit was off him. He scrambled backwards, hitting against a tree. The rabbits circled him again, snarling and baring their teeth.

Hank realized he couldn't rely on Murray, no matter how loud he screamed. He needed to fend off these creatures alone. If only he hadn't dropped his knife. Shoving his hand into his pocket, Hank yanked out the only thing he had, the van keys. Maybe if he was lucky he could catch a few of them in the eye.

Gomer stepped forward, the fur around his mouth wet with blood. A deep rumbling growl reverberated from his chest. Gomer crouched low, prepared to strike. Hank held the keys up, one metal blade sticking through his knuckles, the rest of the chain dangling down and shaking in his hand.

Every pair of red eyes darted to the keys, staring, transfixed at the white keychain. Their mouths twitched and Gomer stepped back, suddenly silent, his eyes holding a note of panic. The rabbits all followed, retreating away from Hank, then bolted off into the darkness.

A shaky breath escaped Hank's mouth, his heart still hammering in his chest. Unclenching his fist, he turned the keys over in his hand, running his fingers over the white keychain. Two weeks ago Murray insisted they stop at the quarter machines on their way out from lunch. He wanted a prize. Here it was still dangling on the key ring, a white rabbit's foot.

"Guess they are good luck," Hank said as he stood and scanned the forest for any sign of brown fur. A breeze wafted through, tossing the leaves in a gentle dance. Everything else was still. Hank hobbled as quickly as his bitten leg would allow, hustling out of the trees.

The van sat where he left it, the most welcome sight Hank had ever seen, even more welcome when he approached and realized Murray wasn't inside. Putting the keys into the ignition, Hank wondered what in the world he would tell Beverly tonight. He spotted Murray's gray shirt almost fifty yards ahead and pulled forward. Murray was crouched down on the ground, a little ball of brown fur wriggling at his feet. Hank fisted what he thought Murray would need, the white poking through his fingers. "Here," he said, tossing Murray the bag of sunflower seeds, his foot releasing the brake. "I wouldn't want anyone to miss out on breakfast."

Arielle Haughee

F ormerly an elementary teacher, Arielle Haughee is an Orlando-based writer with short stories and memoir published in a variety of print and web publications. She focuses on mainstream fiction, speculative fiction, mommy memoir, and children's picture books. Arielle is also active in local critique groups and is a judge in the Royal Palm Literary Award contest.

www.ariellehaughee.com
www.facebook.com/AuthorArielleHaughee
www.amazon.com/Arielle-Haughee/e/B074V9Y9H2

Mato

By Teresa Edmond-Sargeant

He was of an unconventional nature, that Mato. Sure, he was the prototypical black bear, with fur as black as a crow's feathers, paws as huge as, well, the bear claw pastries found in bakery shops, and ears as pointed as the spears that intrepid hunters of long ago used to slaughter his kind. Yet since he was a cub of about six months, after witnessing horrors he of his age was never supposed to witness concerning his parents, Mato ascertained his purpose for existence: to dispel the long-established yet common reputation-maligning stereotypes that he and his kind, the black bear, ate meat. Not only meat such as chicken, beef and pork, but meat of the highest form: human beings.

This bear's teeth mirrored that of the jagged edge of a saw, and his eyes were defiant of any and all obstacles that was unfortunate enough to encounter him, be it a human's bear-proof garbage can set out at the curb in a subdivision only a one-quarter of a mile radius northward of his home, a plant that befell in the bear's way as he went on with his day-to-day activity of poking his nose out of sheer curiosity, or simply taking up the chore of wandering further and further away from those oh-so-horrible humans who had the audacity to set out garbage cans that lock.

One summer morning, Mato lifted his head toward the direction of the sun appearing in the east. This honey-tinted, low-lit glow did its best to push through the edges of the forest's trees, but could only surpass the spaces that the trees didn't cover. Mato blinked his eyes to exercise them into alertness. He pushed up with his forepaws, then straightened his hind legs to raise and level out his body. Mato sniffed through the grass, shifted his head back and forth as if it were steering the rest of his body.

Observing the sun's honey-tinted glow, Mato acknowledged the task up ahead that he must accomplish that morning: hunting through neighborhood after neighborhood, finding any trash can that does not have a bear-resistant lock and find his food that way, all the while maintaining relations between people and black bears with dignity.

Mato followed a dirt path, pondering on the hallmark achievement of his caliber. He engaged the particular walk his favorite path out of all in the woods, for he loved how the path gave way from his home to that of a human couple's home, which was not even one-quarter of a mile. Knowing his home was close to theirs comforted Mato, for it was this arrangement that had him feeling as if they were a family.

Footsteps stomped the dirt ground. Mato stopped. He listened with great intensity at the sound, wondering from what direction the footsteps were coming, how to prepare himself, and what weapons this creature with the footprints may have. The urge to retreat nudged Mato, but at the same time, curiosity propelled him to run up a tree next to him and see what danger – if it was danger – posed to him. He sat on the branch and observed the ground, awaiting the outcome of this situation. Patience was quite a virtue Mato had learned to cull. So much so, the only way he knew how much time had passed was though his observation, with his sharp eyesight, the considerable stretch of a distance the sun had risen.

A second black bear, somewhat larger than Mato yet had a lithe way of moving about on the forest floor, ran across the ground and stopped in front of Mato's tree.

Mato recognized the bear and whispered, "Kiasax?"

The bear named Kiasax moved his head in response to his name being called.

Mato tried again, this time in a sharper whisper: "Kiasax?"

"Mato?" Kiasax looked up and found Mato in the tree.

"Hmm, it's nice to run into your brother again," Kiasax said.

"Keep it down!" Mato controlled his voice but maintained sternness in his pitch.

"As I am happy to see you," Kiasax replied.

"I think there's a human nearby, a hunter. Get up here."

Kiasax approached the tree and, with his sharp claws, ascended the tree and settled high up there with his brother. Mato inclined toward Kiasax's ear, a shining metal clipped in the lobe.

"What are you doing here?" Mato asked. "Last time I saw you, you said you were fleeing to the Panhandle and that was last May."

Kiasax rotated his head toward his brother then at the forest ground, scrutinizing it for the hunter. "What I'm usually good at doing, up there in the Panhandle as well as down here now – stirring up trouble."

"You told me that's why you can't go to my graduation, because state officials were looking for you."

"Ah, yes, graduation. College – The State of Human Scum, if that's the name I recall correctly."

"It's called The State College at Harrison," Mato said.

"So the same day I steal a truck from the state conservation agency, you were graduating with those humans, and there were even more humans with their metal boxes flashing and speaking into those metal sticks. You, the first black bear – the first animal ever! – to be in a human college as a student and not as a taxidermy-prepared specimen. Before I left, what did you tell me you were studying?"

"I majored in public relations and with a minor in international studies."

"Yeah, yeah, you had your hopes on studying black bear rights, but the only curriculum that spoke about black bears was in the sciences. As for my graduation, progress was made that day. That was, until you ruined it!"

Kiasax placed his paw on his chest and cast a solemn glare at Mato.

"There you go again, speaking about black bears' rights as if the words have any meaning to me – to yourself – but I beg your pardon, dear little brother," Kiasax said. "I did not know that graduating with those hairless freaks of nature meant so much to you. The same species who, perhaps two weeks later, will shoot you dead in the woods for no reason other than catching you collecting berries off bushes, which is much more suitable to your nature than going to college. 'I'm sorry I didn't recognize you without your cap and gown, or your school uniform,' they'd say."

Kiasax said the last sentence with the mocking mimicry at what he thought sounded like the typical human voice: a cross between a gargling throat and a whining elephant.

"Then Channel 6 reported that a black bear mauled a human mailman and left him for dead," Mato said. "He survived injuries, but he was left to die. Was it you?"

Kiasax bobbed his head. "'Was it me'?" He scoffed at the question.

"Experts said the bear they caught on camera was tagged." With his snout, Mato indicated toward Kiasax's pierced ear.

"It could be any one of us out there. You know how these humans profile us – we all look the same to them."

"These same experts said they noticed a marking on this bear's forehead." With that comment, Mato moved his same paw toward the left, to Kiasax's forehead. "Seems to me like they got the right bear, or wrong bear, depending on how you look at it," Mato concluded.

"If you'll recall, I didn't get my tag until long after I fled the panhandle. I made my way to South Georgia by then, which was where they tagged me. If I'm captured again, I'll get ..." Kiasax dropped his sentence and looked away. "Well, I won't get into that."

Below the bears, a man appeared wearing an olive-green cap, camouflage from head to toe including a tan vest, leather hiking boots. He brandished a rifle with heightened awareness – at least, that was what he appeared to have to Mato – as the hunter scanned the territory, wondering what could be out there.

Mato took care not to draw attention to himself, so he kept still, being careful not to breath. He also prayed to his gods that Kiasax won't do anything extreme or careless to attract the hunter. Mato anticipated which way or where the hunter would go, and as the hunter stepped to his right, a rustle was heard in the distance. At first, Mato believed that he himself caused a rustling in the tree, but he realized that the noise had emerged from somewhere else. The hunter placed his other foot forward. Soon, he stalked in the direction of the rustle. A gunshot was fired from the direction of where the hunter walked toward, followed by a thump. Mato wasn't sure how much time had passed before hearing that shot fired, but it must have been a long time, he assumed.

The bear brothers anticipated whether the hunter would return. They listened for any clue of the hunter's whereabouts: footsteps, a voice, a rustle of bushes. Yet no sound was emitted. When Mato sensed that the racing of his heart decelerated, he proceeded to throw his leg onto the trunk in preparation of his climbing down, but a paw touched his paw.

"Danger will lurk for you the minute you step into ... their world, understand?" Kiasax said. Empathy and fear choked his voice, and he let go of Mato's paw.

Mato watched as Kiasax retracted his paw, and nodded.

"It's all for freedom," Mato said. "All the civil rights leaders do it: they take risks and most of all, they speak up instead of shutting down. Today may be my day to accomplish that – or at least I can take a step forward in that direction."

Mato crept down the trunk and onto the ground. He walked toward the direction of the sun, determined to get to his destination. A quarter-mile ahead, at the end of his path, was a clearing leading to a cul-de-sac of houses. Mato entered through this opening and noted how, before every single house, there was a trash can displaying the city's seal on its side. Mato approached the first house to his right and knocked over the trash can with his paw. He pounded on the lid's edge, hoping to rip off the lid and nuzzle the contents for some delectable treats only a garbage can offer. After a series of exhausting attempts, Mato gave up and moved on to the next house. Instead of approaching its trash bin, he walked up the pathway and pressed the doorbell with his mighty paw.

Not even 10 seconds later did the door open. A woman of youthful features and a head of tight, brown curls decorated with a red ribbon headband opened the door. She had on a flowing long orange dress with a floral pattern, layered with a white, cropped short-sleeved sweater which was open in the front.

"Mato, it's so good to see you," the woman said smiling, extending her arms and putting them around Mato's neck. She tightened her squeeze and pressed her cheeks against Mato's face.

"Good to see you again, Deanna," Mato said as he passed through the doorway and Deanna closed the door behind him. He thrusted his nose into the air and sniffed it.

"I smell your cooking. It must be delicious, as usual," he said.

"Mato, you say that every week," Deanna said. "I made chocolate chip pancakes. There's also fried eggs, fruits and nuts. I know you'll really eat them up as soon as you sit down at the table."

The two chatted and replied to responses with laughter. They discussed their families, their week had been and even the rainy weather that happened almost every summer day in Central Florida.

Deanna took the lead and Mato followed her down the hall in the kitchen's direction. Throughout Deanna's hallway, political signs leaned against the walls – some were lawns signs, others were posters mounted on boards. Some signs had words and a logo, others only the logo. That logo was a bear's paw print with two vertical rectangles going through them and slightly larger than the paw print.

"Like the campaign signs?" Deanna asked, pointing to one of them with the logo on it as they strolled through the hallway. "It reads 'Pause for bears,' and as you can tell, the symbol of this campaign is a bear's paw. See the two rectangles on it? That is a 'pause' symbol, like if you have a DVR and – well, let me explain what a DVR is first. It's –"

"Yes, Deanna, I know what a 'pause symbol looks like,'" Mato said without giving the interruption so much as a thought.

I hope that didn't come off as too harsh, Mato wondered.

Deanna nodded. "Okay," she said, attempting to get back on a good footing with her statement. "Anyway, 'Pause for Bears' has a double meaning with 'pause' and 'paws' being a homonym. Do you know what a homonym is?"

Deanna was cautious in asking that question, for she didn't know if it would set Mato off. He was aware of this.

"Yes, Deanna, I know what a homonym is. I have been reading human literature since I was a cub. In case you forgot, I made history two months ago as the first black bear to graduate from college."

An awkward silence dwelt between Deanna and Mato, with the latter attempting to understand the dialogue that transpired between them.

Is Deanna as sincere as she is in helping black bears gain their civil rights? It sounds like she doesn't think highly of us.

"To go back to breakfast," Mato said. "It's true that you're a splendid cook, especially since you're one of my favorite humans. I guess not all humans are best at producing waste."

As Deanna reached the kitchen doorway, she stopped and stared at Mato but didn't expound on the reason she had a confused expression, although Mato could only surmise that his comment stung her.

Sizzling was heard from the stove. Deanna approached it, where a frying pan sat on a burner. She lifted a spatula from the counter and flipped the frying egg over.

"Come, sit down," she said, indicating to the head of the kitchen table where an empty chair stood. "There is a bowl of fresh fruits on the table. I know you love you some apples."

Mato nuzzled into the fruit basket on the kitchen table. The sight of oranges, apples, grapes and pears were enough to tempt him into consuming all the fruits (bowl included!). Mato advanced to the table and sat on the floor in front of a stack of chocolate chip pancakes. He stretched his mouth over the stack, and crumbs flaked onto the plate and the table as he devoured the pancakes. He picked up the dish, licked it and dropped it on the table. He sat on his hind legs.

"You just missed Jerry," Deanna said, shutting off the stove. The sizzling continued until it ceased. "He went to the office, and I was going to head to my antique shop. Want to come with me? My staff is great, and, well, maybe in time you can build a relationship with them, bring awareness to them about your civil rights cause."

Deanna removed the empty plate and gave him another one with a new stack, which Mato consumed with glee. He licked the plate and sat back on his hind legs, content with his belly full as he laid a paw on his stomach.

"Deanna, you are a great gatherer – I mean, cook," Mato said.

She laughed. "Thank you, but going back to what I was saying: not only can we get you to do the rounds of doing a black-bear-on-the-street sort of campaign, where you can meet people at my store, but you can go on the campaign trail with Jerry. We'll even make the campaign slogan a hashtag – you know, 'hashtag Pause for Bears,' along with some other hashtags we're putting out there."

Mato looked up with an inquisitive expression. "A hashtag? What's that?"

"Oh, I thought that because you use social media ..."

Mato shook his head. "I heard about this social media, but never used it. A classmate of mine once told me social media is like getting hunted. I said I can't imagine it to be so. He said if you comment on a current event and what you say is different from that of a lot of people's, well, it's equivalent to – and I'm quoting him – "getting your head put in stocks in the public square and the public throwing tomatoes at you." Wow, I didn't know humans punished each other like that, besides the usual wars and murders."

"You should try high school. That's where the brutality really lies. Anyway, a hashtag is like a keyword. If you want a word to trend or if you want to be part of a conversation that's happening online, you put a tic-tac-toe symbol in front of a word, phrase or symbol and your post or tweet will be part of a conversation. Another hashtag we were considering is 'Not all bears.'"

An eyebrow of Mato's poked up with intense curiosity.

"'Not all bears' what, Deanna?" he asked.

"No, no, I wasn't going to say a full sentence. What I mean was with the hashtag 'Not all bears,' it'll get people more aware that, well, not all bears are fill-in-the-blank. Like, if I were to post something online, I'd write, 'hashtag not all bears,' and then the phrase, 'eat people because humans are not black bears' food source.' Something like that. That way, people will be more educated about you and your kind."

Mato nodded. "So that's it? A hashtag and me campaigning with Jerry while he runs for state legislature? Deanna, it's hunting season right now. The last human who ran on a platform on ending the bear hunt, news reports came out that she supported two state bills keeping and expanding hunting season."

"Not every human is the same, just like not every bear is the same." Deanna scooped up the fried egg with the spatula onto her plate, picked out a fork from the silverware drawer and sat down at the table next to Mato.

"I can say with reason that all humans are lying, corrupt murderers who do everything in their power to acquire more of it as well as ... what do you call those objects humans use a lot?" Mato asked. "They're green and resemble lettuce leaves?"

Deanna cut her egg with the fork. She pierced the egg and put it in her mouth. "Money?"

"That's it. Why the fight over something that doesn't care one way or another what you do, or how much blood you shed? Are there more pressing matters out there?"

Deanna finished chewing the egg and swallowed. "There are, but humans are so prone to hurting each other they feed on their emotions and forget their obligations toward one another. They don't remember."

As she reached for an apple in the fruit bowl, a bizarre appetite whetted up within Mato as he watched the apple — no, not the type that would knot the stomach muscles when he's hungry, but a deeper instinct, one that awoke within him a foreign emotion. He couldn't well identify it, but Mato had to pay attention to it, for this emotion might signify a depth which he did not recognize.

He had a sudden craving for ... revenge, in the form of blood. He locked his eyes with the apple while Deanna bit into it. Apple-red blood.

Blood? Impossible. Mato is a black bear – the majority of his diet consisted of plant sources. The rest of his diet consisted of lots of insects and few small animals like armadillos, but certainly not the blood of larger animals and certainly not of humans. Yet why blood?

Keeping his eyes fixated on the apple, Mato spat out another question: "Okay, another question: Why is your husband evil?"

Deanna paused in the middle of taking another bite of her apple. She moved the fruit away from her mouth. "Excuse me?"

"Why *is* he running for state legislature? What is he going to do with sitting at the state capitol, under the rotunda, with his grandstanding about how much he loves bears, and how much he wants to rid the state of the bear hunt because it's the inhumane thing to do?"

Deanna set her apple down on the table and tilted her head at an angle. "You have known me and Jerry for at least two years, since you scared the crap out of us while we were having our picnic date in the woods, but you reassured us right then and there you won't harm us. He's in your corner. He doesn't want anything happening to you or your brother."

"Does he now? With him coming from a family of hunters, I'm not sure how sincere he is."

Mato rolled an apple out of the fruit bowl and sniffed it, imagining chewing on its sweet, crispy contents, but he couldn't help but see, well, red.

"He's a liar, and you're covering for him like a faithful wife should," Mato continued.

"What's with you today?" Deanna shot up from her chair. She paced next to the table, then stopped and faced Mato. "This isn't like you. Now you listen to me: I'm not defending him because he's my husband. I –"

"Like all the others who would cover for their husbands if ever they were caught telling a lie. Jerry Heard may claim to be a black bear rights activist, but I heard he's in the pocket of those who want to expand the state hunt, maybe even take this up to the U.S. Supreme Court!"

"You know, you know way too much about our legal system for a black bear," Deanna said.

"For a black bear? Why shouldn't I?" Mato asked. "Just because I'm a bear, I'm not allowed to understand what our enemies do?"

Mato slammed his paw on the table, flattening the apple. Half of its contents splattered on the table, while the other half flung onto the floor. Deanna jumped back at this action.

"So what am I to you?" Deanna asked. "Am I an enemy too? Do you think we'd treat you the way we did if we thought you were dangerous? Quite the opposite: We know what black bears are really like, and we do what we can to educate the public on how to protect themselves and black bears."

"It's a matter of protecting 'themselves' first, to use your word, right?"

Mato could tell he stumped Deanna with his question, for she cocked her head from side to side and writhed her lips as though doing these actions would jog her brain activity into coming up with what to say next, yet she came up with nothing.

"Well, the reason we have the bear hunt is because of conservation reasons," she said. "Bears tend to — well, they tend to breed like crazy unless something is done to keep them in check."

"Are you saying all bears are prone to breeding too much, without any ability to control their sexual urges or their wanting to reproduce whatsoever?"

Deanna skewed her lips and her cheeks contorted. "Well, you're ... animals. You live by instinct; you go by your base desires. You're ... not humans."

Mato's patience was decreasing. He stalked toward her. "That is a very unfair stereotype, one that is pure propaganda used to slander us so black bears and humans can't live in harmony. You have to understand this civil rights activism is tough. You must know, you're – what are you? Your species?"

"Among humans, we don't have species; we have races." Deanna's voice was clipped as she emphasized that statement. "I myself am what we call a black American."

"Ah, yes, black American – you have told me stories about how your ancestors were owned by other humans that were white, and how your people fought to get free. Then there was this tall, lanky man responsible for making it a reality. What's his name, the one I saw in photographs wearing a tail coat and top hat?"

"Abraham Lincoln?"

Mato nodded. "Yes, him."

Deanna turned her head away from Mato and scrunched her nose, sniffing. "Mato?" She sniffed again. "Do you smell that?"

Mato sniffed also. "I think I do, now that you mention it."

With a drastic and desperate swing-around at the waist, Deanna glimpsed at the stove, but saw it was off. "It can't be the stove, so nothing's burning."

White wisps streamed outside in front of a kitchen window. Mato reared his head and nudged Deanna with his nose: "Deanna, look outside!"

Deanna saw what Mato saw outside and gasped. She rushed outside, with Mato following. Once there, they halted. Deanna nearly stumbled backwards at what they encountered: five bears – four males and one female. One male bear in front of this group had a closed scar, where an eye would have been. He also had a tag in one of his ears. All were next to a smoking pile of wood at the base of the house. The pile soon caught fire, and the flame's sparks leaped onto the house.

"Kiasax!" Mato called out. Then in a lower volume, he said, "Kiasax, don't do this. She is not like other humans. She's different!"

"The only thing that's different about her is she'll let a black bear into her house!" Kiasax cried out. "All that is an elaborate trap she's laying out to exterminate you – and us!"

Mato ran past Deanna and threw himself onto his brother. Both wrestled on the grass, their claws ripping into one another's fur and flesh. They knocked over the barbecue grill and patio furniture before tumbling into the side of the house. No matter where they tumbled onto or into what area of the yard they tussled, they continued to claw and bite at each other.

Kiasax bore his sharp teeth and with them, gashed into the front of Mato's neck. It was like bear vampirism. Blood squirted out of Mato's neck and onto Kiasax's teeth, mouth, and face. Kiasax released Mato and stepped back with flesh hanging from his mouth. He spit it out at a few feet from where the brothers fought, at the staircase where Deanna still lingered. Mato fell onto his back. Blood continued to spill from his neck and on the grass.

Deanna gasped. She glimpsed over at the fire, which by that time, had spread along the bottom of the house.

"There is no need to fight," Deanna said. "We're doing everything we can to unite humans and black bears – educating people about you, your nature, what people can do when they encounter one, all that."

Kiasax flashed his eyes at Deanna; they were glossed with redness.

"You're correct – we're not carnivorous by nature," Kiasax said, "but we are out for blood, nonetheless. We will rise up, and overtake this neighborhood – garbage cans and humans be damned! We will storm the State

House, and Storm the federal Supreme Court to make them know we bears will not be taken for granted, and that you can't take our hides as trophies."

Deanna backed upward on the stairs, onto the deck. "You don't have to do that! They'll end the bear hunt next week and they might not even have one next year. I heard in the news that state conservations found the bear population is under control –"

The bears growled at Deanna as they surrounded her on the deck. Each bear, with their eyes like small, black onyx, glared at her, intensity rising within each of them as they prepared to be on the offensive.

"If we must use violence to achieve peace, then that is what we must do," Kiasax said. "There is nothing you can do to stop us."

With that, the bears circled Deanna and closed in on her. Her screams were stifled by the bears' growls, followed by silence on her part as Mato listened to the bears' claws ripped into flesh. He struggled to get up and stop the madness and save Deanna, but his lack of strength forced his eyes closed.

"Pause for bears," he mumbled with his last breath. "Pause ... for ... bears."

Teresa Edmond-Sargeant

Teresa Edmond-Sargeant is an award-winning journalist, author, poet, ghostwriter, and editor.

As a newspaper staff writer in North Jersey, Edmond-Sargeant won two N.J. Press Association awards. She also received an award from the Florida Press Association as a reporter for a Central Florida community newspaper.

She is the author of the poetry book "How Fate's Confusion Connects" and many Amazon Kindle short story ebooks.

She graduated from Fairleigh Dickinson University, Teaneck, N.J., with a bachelor's degree in communication. She got her certification in advanced fiction writing from the Adult Learning Center of Osceola, Kissimmee, Fla.

She is a member of the Florida Writers Association.

When she is not working, she enjoys spending time with family and friends, reading, working out, shopping, and traveling.

www.teresa-edmond-sargeant.com
www.Facebook.com/teresasedmondsargeant
www.twitter.com/teresaesargeant
www.amazon.com/teresasedmondsargeant

Baa Baa Black Sheep

By G. H. Finn

"….the wolf in sheep's clothing…"
"…the wolf in the fold…"
From the Fable by Aesop (born 620–died 560 BC)

"Be ye war of fals prophetis,
that comen to you in clothing is of scheep,
but withynneforth thei ben as wolues of raueyn."
Gospel of Matthew, 7:15, John Wyclif's translation, 1382

The farm had been peaceful once. Until the awful events began, a year and a month ago. It had been thirteen moons since the night of the attack, down in the valley below Wulfherd's Hill.

Old farmer Shuckshank, the owner of Coldfarthing Farm, had been lucky that night. The night of the wolf. The long night of teeth and claws. And terror. And death. And Wool.

Red, bloody wool.

Giles Shuckshank had been asleep when it happened. He was old and doddering and rarely left his bed these days. So, he didn't see his sheep being killed. But his granddaughter did.

Young Florence Shuckshank, known as Flossy to her friends and family, had been awake that night. Just turned seventeen, she was clever enough and pretty enough to be well liked in the village, getting wolf-whistles from the boys, even if some of the older folk criticized her fashionable clothes and bright make-up. "Mutton dressed as lamb, that one," they said. But Flossy took no notice.

She was still up, not long back home from a trip to the cinema in Ulfston. The night the flock was slaughtered. Flossy swore they were killed by a wolf.

Most of the everyday country folk said it must have been an insane Border Collie that attacked the sheep. Maybe a mad Malamute. Or perhaps a deranged Alsatian. Possibly a psychotic Husky.

They thought Flossy's description of the savage creature was nonsense. Make-believe. The girl was crying wolf to get attention. Or sympathy. Or because she was upset at the loss of the sheep. She had jumped at shadows, that was all.

True, the county's folklore *was* filled with tales of wolves, some that hunted on four legs, and some that walked on two. But they were just shaggy dog stories, weren't they? Nothing to take *seriously*. It couldn't have been a *wolf* that killed the sheep. That was silly. There had been no wolves in Britain for hundreds of years.

But the villagers hadn't been there. They weren't at the farm when it happened. They didn't see it. They didn't *know*.

In the pub, the regulars were more poetic. They were usually as poetic as newts. They waxed lyrical.

They said it was a great ghostly hound. A devil dog. A monster. A demon.

They were closer to the truth than they realized.

Flossy Shuckshank had shot the beast. She'd killed the wolf. Or rather, she'd *thought* she had. She had certainly tried to. Flossy couldn't imagine how it could possibly have survived. She'd hit it with both barrels from her grandfather's shotgun, hastily grabbed from its hanging place above the mantelpiece. Flossy was a good shot. She had a keen eye. And it was easy to see the wolf in the pale, bright, full moonlight.

The blast *should* have blown its head off. And yet somehow it had still managed to run away, into the darkness of the night.

But not before it killed the sheep. The whole flock. All of them.

Well, *almost* all. There had been *one* survivor.

A little lamb. A tiny, black, woolly, baby sheep. It had been bitten, but not badly. Though it lost its mother.

Over the next few weeks, Flossy looked after him. The baby ram. The little orphaned lamb. She felt sorry for him, and decided to keep him as a pet. She joked that he was the black sheep of the family. How right she was.

In the day's following the great slaughter at the farm, Flossy came to love her little lamb.

She thought about calling him Rama, after the Hindu god.

Or Ramesses, like the Egyptian pharaoh.

But eventually she named him Ramsey.

For his part, Ramsey loved Flossy too. In fact, he adored her. She took him everywhere. He trotted along behind her, happily bleating a greeting whenever she looked at him or stroked his fuzzy, little woolly head.

Old Giles Shuckshank didn't much like his granddaughter doting on the creature, but aside from a muttered grumble he said nothing. Flossy more or less ran the farm these days, and he knew he wasn't much company for her. He shrugged and went back to bed with a bottle of whiskey to keep him warm.

The sight of Flossy walking along with the small sheep trailing behind her soon became familiar in the village. Most of the villagers thought it was sweet, the way she girl and the sheep doted on one another. But a few of the older inhabitants said it was unnatural.

"That thing follows her about like a dog. It ain't right," one ancient codger muttered, crossing himself with a shaking hand. "No good will come of it."

"She looks like a witch with a familiar sent by the Devil himself," tutted his wizened, white-haired wife, "The black beast has the mark of Satan on in, right enough."

Flossy scowled at the gossiping busy-bodies, said loudly, "Baa! Humbug!" Then she scooped little Ramsey up in her arms, and hurried home.

Time passed and the sheep grew. As the moon above waxed and waned, the months went by and the little lamb soon became a fine young ram. Its woolly black fleece glistened, and strong horns curled gracefully above its happy, proud head. Flossy and the sheep became inseparable, both loving each other dearly, always delighted to be in each other's company.

All was peaceful again, as the wheel of the seasons turned around.

It was almost the anniversary of the great slaughter.

Then one night, unexpectedly, there was a sudden disturbance in the sheep fold.

Flossy could see the sheep clearly from the kitchen window, it was only one night before the full moon and the pale moonlight illuminated the farm brightly. The sheep were running about frantically, as though in fear of some unknown menace. Flossy rushed out to check on them. Ramsey had become exceptionally skittish. He usually lived in his own small pen, with some ewes to keep him company, away from the rest of the flock. He was there now, but all the other sheep were avoiding him, staying as far away from him as the pen they would allow. Flossy was worried about her lovely ram. More than just a pet, he was her best friend. She loved him.

Far from his usual, cheerful self, the jet-black ram paced about inside the fold, bleating mournfully at the moon.

It's almost as though he can remember what happened. Flossy thought, and bent to stroke the young sheep, now almost fully an adult, trying to comfort and reassure him. Without warning, Ramsey snapped at her arm. His big chunky teeth drew blood, and Flossy drew her hand back quickly, more in shock than pain. The sheep had bitten her finger! Ramsey had *never, ever,* behaved like this. She went quickly back to the kitchen to wash her cut and find a plaster, upset and worried about the poor, frightened animal.

But the next day, as the sun rose over the valley, Ramsey was once again his usual cheerful self, nuzzling adoringly against Flossy's thigh and baaing his affection. She stroked his woolly head lovingly, glad and relieved that he was back to normal. She had to go to the post office that morning, and was pleased the young sheep could come with her. So they set off, walking and trotting merrily together in the warm sunshine. A brightly smiling young woman striding cheerfully, with her happy ram gamboling along behind her.

As Flossy passed the playground of the village school, a few of the children there called out to her. They said she was just like *"Mary"* from the old nursery rhyme.

"Except," said one girl, "your little lamb didn't have a fleece as white as snow."

One of the boys immediately started singing, somewhat tunelessly,

Flossy, Flossy,
Had a Lamb.
Its wool was black as night.
And anywhere
That Flossy went
That lamb would cause a fright.

A wide-eyed girl immediately began to croon,
Baa, Baa, Black Sheep,
What's beneath your wool?
Will there be more death and blood,
When the moon is full?

The children gathered in a circle around Flossy and Ramsey.
Another child sang,
One, two, three-four-five,
Once she caught a sheep alive,
Six, seven, eight-nine-ten,
Will it ever let her go again?
Why won't it let her go?
Because it bit her finger so!
What will happen from that bite?
Death and terror in the night!

Then all the children in the circle chorused together,
Little Flo, creep
Beside your sheep,
Who knows what lurks inside it?
Leave it alone,
And it will come home,
Dragging the dead things behind it.

Flossy laughed at the children. They were always making up daft rhymes. Although, those particular songs were more than a little... unusual. Peculiar. Her brow creased a little as she watched the blank staring eyes of the children, gazing fixedly at her and the sheep. But she shook her head and dismissed it, turning away and heading for the post office, with Ramsey's cloven hooves clip-clopping behind her.

The next night, Saturday, seven sheep were killed. All the ewes that lived with Ramsey were dead. Torn to pieces.

On the Sunday morning, Ramsey's sheep-fold was filled with paw-marks in the mud. Not like the prints of the sheep's hooves, these prints were clearly canine. And huge. The villagers would probably say it was a dog again. But Flossy knew better. These were wolf tracks. She was beside herself with fear and worry, until she found her young ram alive but cowering behind the water trough. He was shaking and shivering and covered in blood. He'd tried to hide himself, away in the far corner of the fold. Luckily, he was unhurt. Flossy let out a great sigh of relief, and began to wash the worst of the blood from his curly black wool.

That damned wolf has returned, she thought, and looking around at the slaughter, she began to plot revenge. *The moon will be full tonight*, she thought, *I'll wait with the shotgun. It won't escape again.*

That evening she propped herself up by the kitchen window, sitting in an old armchair with the shotgun on her lap. Her grandfather was in a drunken stupor, asleep in his bed upstairs. She'd made a jug of coffee to keep herself awake. She had the radio on. It was just some boring religious broadcast but she couldn't be bothered to get up and change the station. Her eyes were glued to the scene outside the window. Watching. Waiting.

Flossy woke with a start. She hadn't realized that she'd nodded off. The voice on the radio was droning on in a dull monotone, reciting a Biblical passage. She heard the voice of a vicar say,

"The passage reads, 'Beware of false prophets, which come to you in sheep's clothing, but inwardly they are ravening wolves.'–That's from Matthew 7:15, in the King James version of 1611."

Suddenly, from outside, came the sounds of some commotion. Flossy panicked a little. She was worried about Ramsey. She'd had half a mind to bring him into the kitchen with her, just to be on the safe side, but eventually she decided he'd be secure enough in his pen, all alone now his companions were dead, but with Flossy watching over him armed with the shotgun. The farm's other sheep were in separate enclosures. From the sound of the bleating, they were becoming agitated. Something was frightening them.

Flossy quietly got up and opened the kitchen door, peering out into the farmyard, cradling the shotgun carefully.

Everything looked normal, apart from the sheep milling about in fear. Flossy couldn't see what they were afraid of. She was worrying about the sheep, and wondering what was worrying them. They were all bleating frantically now. All except Ramsey.

He stood alone in the center of his hold, staring up at the moon. Flossy thought Ramsey would be bleating to, but unlike all the other sheep, he made no sound. Flossy was a little unnerved by that. There seemed something almost unnatural about it. Uncanny. She felt disturbed by the silence of the lamb.

And then, as Flossy watched from the kitchen doorway, the full moon shone down on Ramsey. Without warning, the black sheep began to change. She saw the young ram clearly, standing alone in the moonlight.

Ramsey began to swell, growing in size. He bleated pitifully as his limbs elongated and twisted. His curly wool fell away, the fleece sliding off his flesh, first showing muscles and bones only then to reveal thick fur sprouting out beneath. The *thing* that had been a sheep grew until it was massive. Hideous and terrible. Before her terrified gaze, Ramsey became a monster. No longer hidden in sheep's clothing, her little lamb became a wolf. Had Flossy not seen the transformation, she might have taken the demonic beast to be a true wolf, albeit one of awful size. But then the *thing* stood upright, poised on its hind legs. It stood with a crooked posture, its back hunched and its forelegs raised. Its paws were tipped with scimitar-like claws. It stepped deliberately forward, walking on two legs, then turned its grizzled head in Flossy's direction. It sniffed toward her with its canine snout, while staring straight at the young woman. Its eyes were big as saucers. Yellow orbs glowed from a cruel face covered in matted black fur. Its fang-filled maw gaped wide, letting a long red tongue hang out from the monstrous mouth. It grinned with a bestial smile. A smile that eagerly promised blood, pain and death.

Flossy didn't know what to think. Or what to do. But she forced herself to step outside, away from the kitchen, out into the night.

She stood in the pale, bright light of the full moon and began to raise the shotgun, only to drop the weapon to the ground as she felt a hideous pain pulse through her body.

Waves of agony hit her as her limbs twisted madly. Her feet burst out through her Wellington boots, replaced by cloven hooves. Her hair began to curl and turn to wool, tufts erupting through her skin, spreading across her entire body. Her clothes tore and split at the seams as her woolly limbs stretched them past endurance.

Flossy stared at the moon and her throat erupted with an uncanny, eldritch, eerie sound...

"Bbbbbaaaaaaaaaaarrrrrggghhh! Bbbaaaaaaaarr! Baaaaaaaaaaaaggggh!" She bleated beneath the pale light of the full moon.

A part of her mind retained enough humanity to realize what had happened. Ramsey, when just a tiny lamb, had been the only survivor of the original slaughter. He had been bitten, but he had lived. He had survived not the bite of a wolf, but of a *werewolf*. The bite of that unholy werewolf must have passed on its demonic infection to the baby lamb, but the curse had not shown itself until the sheep was full-grown. Until then, Ramsey had not been capable of shapeshifting into a monster. But nevertheless, he had been a *carrier* of the curse. And Ramsey had bitten her!

When Ramsey had bitten Flossy's finger, he had passed on his dormant lycanthropy. It spread to her like a demonic infection, and the terrible taint then lurked unknown within her blood. Without releasing it, Flossy, like Ramsey before her, had become infected with a metamorphic and devilish form of possession. She too had been stricken by the diabolically viral curse.

Now, tonight, beneath the light of the full moon, poor little Ramsey had at last become a *sheepwolf*.

And when Flossy had herself stood in the moonlight, the hideous curse that had been waiting since Ramsey bit her, biding its time until the full moon, had now transformed her into an unholy *weresheep*.

Flossy knew that was what she had become. Unnatural instincts coursed through her body, mind and soul. She wanted to find a tranquil, unsuspecting pasture, to hunt down virgin grass and tear it to shreds. Her greatest desire was to pounce upon an innocent plant, bite its succulent foliage and chew it to bits. Oh, the joy she would feel as green sap dripped from her savage teeth! "Bbbbbaaaaaaaaaaaaa!!!!!" She bleated again, with a diabolic frenzy.

But then a small part of Flossy's mind recognized a danger. The weresheep sniffed the air, turned and saw the sheepwolf staring at her. Hungrily.

Flossy let out a squeak, "Oh flock!" she bleated, and turned to run as fast as her cloven feet would carry her. The sheepwolf followed, panting at her hooflike heels.

The human side of Flossy's mind made her want to pause to grab the fallen shotgun, but she knew that her hoof-hands could never manage to work the trigger. Then her new sheeplike instincts took over and she headed away from the house, running across the farmyard wildly. The sheepwolf growled behind her, snapping at her dainty and fleetly scampering cloven hooves.

Panicking, Flossy ran toward an empty sheepfold, an old unused pen fenced in with thick wooden beams. She did her best to try to squeeze her woolly bulk through the wooden struts around the pen, struggling to get through to the other side. She almost made it, but the ravening sheepwolf mercilessly snarled and snapped, biting her on a hind leg, just as she managed to wriggle into the pen.

Flossy felt the bite but did her best to ignore it. Her human mind wasn't working properly as her new sheeplike instincts began to take over. She tried her best to concentrate but her thoughts were woolly and all she could do was stand and cower in the pen.

A monstrous wolflike terror slavered behind her. The devilish beast that had once been her lovely little ram howled in frustration as it tried to force its hugely muscled bulk through the gap in the fence, frantic in its desire to reach Flossy and tear her limb from limb. But the horror that had once been Ramsey was too big to squeeze through the gap in the wooden fence. It was stuck.

But not for long. Flossy could see that it was huffing and puffing with effort. In moments, it would break the fence into splinters. She wanted to run away, but instead, in her terror, the weresheep did a most unsheeplike thing. Whether from courage or desperate fear, she forced herself to step forward on her shaking hooves and, with her big blocky teeth, she bit the snarling demon-wolf on the end of its big black nose. It howled in pain and rage.

But rather than deterring the possessed beast, the bite merely seemed to make it even more determined to sink its fangs into Flossy's woolly throat.

Quaking with terror and bleating with fear, she stepped back, edging away from the darkness that enfolded the sheepwolf, until she reached the far side of the pen and stood quivering in a patch of moonlight. With an ear-splitting crash, the weresheep shattered the thick wooden fence and howled in demonic triumph.

As she stood in the moonlight, another weird sensation began to course through Flossy's body. The blood in her veins felt like it was on fire. Her limbs twisted and she doubled over in pain. A small part of her brain wondered what was happening. *I feeeellll liiiikkke I'mmm beeeeeiiinng bleaten blaaaack and blluuuueee,* she thought as a new transformation came over her.

While her hind-legs retained their cloven hooves, her forelegs twisted and her hands became paws. Hooves dropped away as she sprouted claws. Thick fur burst forth on her back, mingling with the curling wool. Her large chunky teeth were pushed aside as huge sharp fangs thrust their way between them. She lifted her head and let out an awful, echoing, eldritch cry, "HooooowwwwlllllllbaaaaaOooooooooobbbbbaaaaaaaaahhoooowwwlllllll"

Dimly, in the dark recesses of her mind, Flossy realized what had happened. Ramsey, now an awful sheepwolf, had bitten her again as she'd struggled into the empty pen.

When Ramsey, in his usual sheep form, had first bitten her, the metamorphic curse had forced her to transform into a woolly monster – half-woman, half-sheep. A *weresheep.* Or perhaps more properly a *wif*sheep, as she was female.

But then, after his transformation into a sheepwolf, Ramsey had bitten her again.

Now Flossy had a double-dose of the curse.

She had altered once more into a *thing* that was part woman, part sheep and part wolf.

A werewolfsheep.

Or sheepwerewolf.

Or weresheepwolf.

Or sheepwolfwoman.

Or something like that anyway.

Bizarre instincts fought against each other, each overwhelming the next. Flossy wanted to scream. And to howl. And to bleat. She wanted to eat grass and drink blood and have a nice cup of tea. She put her paws to her head as her hooves gave way beneath her, falling to the ground to shudder in a growling, baaing, wailing heap.

Huge glowing eyes watched her, hungrily.

The slavering jaws of the sheepwolf dripped sticky saliva as it padded menacingly toward the stricken Flossy, eager to sink its cruel fangs into her undefended throat.

But as it reached her and stood over the prostrate Flossy, preparing to feast bloodily on its helpless victim, the light of the full moon once more broke through the clouds above and shone down upon the monster.

Suddenly a throbbing pain filled its snout.

The sheepwolf's nose was still sore from where it had been bitten by the weresheep. And now a new sensation spread out, racing though its body. It howled in demonic fury as its hind legs grew hooves. The coarse fur that covered its lupine head was pushed aside as huge, curling horns thrust up from its skull, between its pointed ears. Wool curled across its back. It howled and baaed in pain and anger.

And then yet *another* transformation began. Paws became hands. Its canine teeth fell, both fur and wool disappeared from its head, only to be replaced by a pale pink human face. The weresheep's bite had turned it part human.

The misshapen monster fell to his knees, crying, bleating and growling in confusion and pain.

Flossy struggle onto all fours and crawled, painfully, over to the suffering *thing*.

It looked up at her and both distorted creatures recognized that now they were each exactly the same. They were a pair of weresheepwolves.

"Ohhh myyyy poooOOOOrrrr Ramseyyyyy." Flossy howled, bleatingly.

Ramsey managed to struggle up into a sitting position, and put a comforting hand onto Flossy's paw, then patted her on the head and amid growls and baas he whispered, in a deep manly voice, "Oh my dear Flossy… How happy I am to touch your wool and stroke your fur."

Flossy looked sensuously into Ramsey's big eyes, seeing herself reflected there. Part sheep, part wolf, but all woman.

"Ramsey." she said, longingly.

Ramsey looked at her wolfishly, and smiling, said, "I love ewe."

Flossy looked at Ramsey lovingly. She wasn't at all sure how everything would work out, but in her heart, she was sure that she and Ramsey would manage. *Somehow.*

As long as they had each other. As long as they were together.

Even if it was only once a month, under the light of the glowing full moon.

G. H. Finn

G. H. Finn is the pen name of someone who keeps his real identity secret to escape the eternal wrath of the ever vengeful eldritch Elder Gods. And to avoid library fines.

Having written non-fiction for many years, Finn began writing fiction in 2015, and currently has around 50 short stories in various stages of publication. He especially enjoys mixing genres (sometimes in a blender, after beating them insensible with a cursed rolling pin) including mystery, horror, steampunk, sword-and-sorcery, dark comedy, fantasy, detective, dieselpunk, weird, supernatural, sword-and-planet, speculative, folkloric, Cthulhu mythos, sci-fi, spy-fi, satire and urban fantasy.

ghfinn.orkneymagic.com
www.facebook.com/g.h.finn
www.twitter.com/GanferHaarFinn
UK www.amazon.co.uk/G-H-Finn/e/B0147L6E66/
US www.amazon.com/G-H-Finn/e/B0147L6E66/

Sassy Larue Descends Into Hell For A Bottle of Milk

By J. P. Dildine

Sassy Larue was a dog. Sassy Larue was no ordinary dog. Sassy Larue was a Min-Pin with a deep-seated love and biological tolerance for sweet milk which, in that moment, Sassy lapped at with fierce abandon. Sassy's life, up until a week ago, had been bliss. Sassy's doting mom was a human named Liza who from the time Sassy was a young pup had treated Sassy as an equal. She shared the bed with Sassy who had her own pillow. Sassy liked laying on the cushy bag of feathers, listening to the labored breathing of her mommy and taking in the aroma of whatever desserts they had indulged in before bed. Sassy loved licking Liza's tears off her plump, rosy cheeks as Liza lamented her loneliness. Sassy tolerated the men who seemed to come and go. None of them stayed for long. So far, Dave had been her favorite. He always came into the house smelling of corned beef and doling out regular head scratches. Sassy Larue liked that one. One time, while Dave was making Liza happy, she dug her small, black, furry face into his pants pocket as they lay on the floor and discovered a world of interesting crumbs.

Unfortunately, Dave stopped coming over, and Sassy had to work harder than ever before to cheer up her mommy. As Liza went on and on about Dave and how he had to go back to someone named Wife, Sassy tried to distract her from her pain by prancing around on her back legs, but it was no use. Liza was depressed for a long time, and although Sassy liked the fact that they ate a wider array of sugar based products, she wished her mommy could see how amazing she was even without a man in her life.

So, when the beast named Hank came into the picture, Sassy put up with him. Hank, the large turd who moved in last night after only two dates. Hank, who on the first date said he hated dogs, especially small dogs. Hank, the fat guy who on the second date told Liza her treadmill was dusty. Hank, whose loud, obnoxious voice boomed throughout the apartment.

"This mutt is a hot mess, Liza. You don't feed dogs milk. It's gonna shit for days." Hank cracked his chubby fingers as he spoke aloud to an empty room. "Seriously, Liza, I don't know what the hell you're thinking, but dogs are not people. People are people. Dogs are animals. It just doesn't make any sense how you do things around here."

Hank smacked his lips a bit causing the small white spittle webs in the corners of his mouth to yo-yo up and down. He leaned with his arm up against the doorway of the kitchen like a much skinnier man, his bulbous pot belly with stretch marks clearly visible from underneath his black t-shirt with a picture of Einstein on its front. Sassy looked up from her bowl and saw that Hank was glaring at her. Sassy moved her eyes downward to the crazy haired man on his shirt. Even he mocked her with his tongue out. Sassy Larue got a shiver and then went back to lapping up the sweet milk.

Hank shook his head and called out in the direction of the bedroom. "Jesus, Liza, are you hearing me?"

"Yes, baby, I do. I'm sorry. I'm just running late to work," Liza called from the messy bathroom in the back.

"Look, I think I'm gonna rearrange a few things in the living room today."

"Oh. Uh, okay," Liza hollered back, unsure.

"Hey, don't think I forgot about last night," Hank reminded her.

Liza stopped brushing her wiry hair in front of the mirror for a moment as she thought about their evening together the night before and let out a sigh. "I know. I'm sorry. I promise I won't do it again."

Hank smacked his lips, dropped his arm as he leaned his back against the entryway. "I told you. You can come, you can listen, but do not try to interrupt our flow."

"I know, I know, I'm so sorry," she said pulling with a bit more force on her hair. Hank patted his belly gently as he moved his head side to side to stretch.

"Look, it's ok. You didn't cost us the game, but just remember, if history is not your forte, or sports, or anything useful, well then, just shut it. You confused Tommy, and he sided with your answer because you have tits, and that caused dissention amongst the ranks. I've spent a long time cultivating my crew, and we could have won, but you two blew it," Hank's reprimanding continued.

"Didn't we wind up in 5th place?" Liza reminded him with a light voice.

Hank wasn't going to let it go. "Not the point, Liza. It disrupted the flow, and we never recovered," said Hank as he glanced toward the bookshelf in the far corner of the living room displaying a trophy from years ago.

The trophy, a small samurai sword sitting on the small wooden arms of a plaque said "Nakatomi Trivia Contest: First Place". Hank loved that trophy. He made sure he dusted it several times a day, and when no one was looking, he'd take the short, surprisingly sharp sword out and make believe he was slicing and dicing the competition. On one occasion, to win a bet, he sliced a beer can in clean, symmetrical halves with infomercial-like speed.

Liza breezed into the room, her business suit jacket a bright, baby blue that matched her eyeshadow. She went right up to Hank with a smile on her face. "I'll make it up to you. Pork chops and turnip greens tonight?"

Hank raised an eyebrow and gave a snide smile. "You were gonna make that anyway."

He grabbed her hand hard and pulled her closer, catching her off guard. As he brought her body in toward his, he reached up and grabbed her face, squeezing hard enough to make her round cheeks push up. Foreheads touching, he pulled her free hand down to his crotch. Liza opened her hand willingly and embraced the front of his jeans. Her eyes looked down. "Look at me," he softly demanded. Her eyes met his. "Later, you're gonna make up for this in all kindsa ways." His unusually bulging eyes gawked at her heaving breasts, and Liza's eyes followed his. He met her gaze. "After I tie up and spank those double F's, you're gonna sprain that jaw from how hard I work you."

Sassy turned her attention from the milk, confused by the vibe in the room. Sassy sensed both fear and longing. She growled halfheartedly with her brown tipped black ears pointing slightly backwards.

"I gotta go, baby," Liza mumbled from her smooshed face.

Hank turned to the low growling from the dog. "Oh yeah, fucktard? What are you gonna do about it?"

"Please, baby, I gotta go," came Liza's muffled request.

Hank didn't turn his eyes from the dog.

"Yeah, yeah," he said and let go of her.

Liza straightened her jacket as Hank went to the front door and opened it for her. She grabbed her keys off the key hanger that had a picture of puppies playing in tall grass with the caption "Who Let the Dogs Out". Sassy followed her into the living room and sat as she had many times before to watch Liza leave.

"Love you, honey bear," Liza said to her eager Sassy whose stubby tail wiggled with fury. Liza walked towards the door and said, "Love you too, my big honey bear."

As she went in for a kiss on Hank's lips, he turned his head and gave her his cheek.

"Lipstick," he complained.

"Sorry." She sheepishly smiled as she tried to wipe off the mark. Hank waved her off. Liza walked out the door while Hank rubbed the red splotch.

"Remember," he called out as she walked away, "it ain't gonna suck itself."

Liza giggled as she hurried off to her car.

Sassy Larue decided right then and there. Hank had to die.

Sassy Larue wanted to vacate her bowls without the loud, annoying ramblings coming from the giant moron on the phone who held her leash. Sassy usually enjoyed the intoxicating smells from the fence line grass. It solidified, for her, the knowledge that she was not alone and that the army of fellow species whose fertilizer reached up into her nose, touching her very soul, meant she was part of a tribe—an ancient species. It was sacred time when she got to leave a return message for all who came after her. This was time when, in normal circumstances, Liza would look down on her with quiet esteem and gentle encouragement. This was a time that Sassy looked forward to with excitable anticipation, but it was now being ruined by the amoeba with opposable thumbs named Hank. Hank paid no attention to Sassy, pulling and tugging her to-and-fro as he walked back and forth talking to someone heatedly, perhaps having an argument–an argument Sassy hoped he was losing.

"Of course, I meant Voodoo economics, dumbass. Supply side economics and Voodoo economics are the same thing. Why are you so dumb, Tommy?" Hank took a hard one-hundred-eight-degree march in the opposite direction of Sassy.

The small dog heard tiny bells and turned to get a glimpse of Gilda, the old lady from the condo above theirs. It looked like she was emptying boxes of plant stems into the compost dump as she hummed an old tune, 'Puttin On the Ritz'. Every time she moved her feet, the tiny bells on the anklet she wore rang sweetly. Gilda smiled at the dog. Sassy liked her.

The leash tightened and the millisecond Hank felt tension in the line, he yanked hard causing Sassy to yelp as she was forced into the air, landing on her side and working to get her legs underneath her. Suddenly, Gilda's sweet humming stopped.

"Hey!!" A voice yelled out.

Hank continued rambling, oblivious. "Let me tell you, if they don't get more knowledgeable judges, we will take our game elsewhere, the fucktards."

"Hey!! Michael Vick, I'm talking to you!!" Hank's frustration turned into annoyance even though he wasn't totally sure he was the one being talked to.

Gilda stood furrow browed with one aged fist balled up, and the other hand gripping rotting plant remains. "You tug like that on that dog again, Mister Meany, and I'll show you the trap door to hell!"

Hank told Tommy to hold on then held the phone to his chest. He tongued the inside of his cheek in amused pondering. "Lady, do you have an issue?"

"Yessiree, I do," said Gilda in her southern drawl. "That precious beast is a blessing, young man. A gift of the Goddess who deserves all the respect and mercy thereof."

Hank shook his head in disbelief, taking a moment to run through his mind of random facts. "Listen, maaaaam, this ANIMAL is a domesticated canine which has been selectively bred over a millennia to enhance certain genetic traits through inbreeding that eventually became this short, little, purse-fitting, brown piece of shit. So, no make-believe Goddess or other delusion-induced manmade being created it—we did! Some fucktard with an animal fetish, so don't lecture me."

Gilda's frustration and anger melted away as she cocked her head sideways. Sweetly, she mocked him. "Oh, I know your kind. There have always been men like you. Arrogant, short sighted, smug men who are so preoccupied with their own existence, reading too much Nietzsche, and lording over others to make up for their own shortcomings. Creepy crawlers like you need to be squashed, Mr. Meany."

"Whatever, hag," Hank said dismissively as he turned away and resumed the one-way conversation he was dominating.

Sassy looked back at Gilda. Gilda stared a hole through Hank's back as he walked away, but then she looked at Sassy and gave her a reassuring look.

Gilda smiled and quietly said, "Don't worry, sugar, it's all gonna be alright."

Sassy liked Gilda.

After they got back into the apartment, Hank continued his tirade over the phone. "Look, I want you guys over here at 6:30 to practice. No, I don't want to go over to Frank's place. It smells like piss. Now that I've got this place, we're gonna work over here. Nah, she doesn't care. I'll make her whip us some grub and pick up beers."

Ms. Larue felt the pressure in her bowels. She'd never had time to leave her return message outside. Sassy was filled with resentment. As Hank walked back and forth on the carpet barking orders at the sad sap on the other line, Sassy angled herself and allowed the process to begin. Normally, she would never do such a thing, but the idea of watching him pick up her biological memo excited her. Hank was oblivious until the first scented molecules hit his nose. By then, the deed had already been done. He looked down at the pile and standing close by was the steadfast dog who stared up at him without blinking.

"Mother fucker!" Hank kicked at Sassy, missing as she moved swiftly out of the way. He was off balance now, and couldn't help but squarely slam his foot directly down into the center of the mess. "FUCK!" He danced on one foot, trying to avoid putting his contaminated foot on the carpet.

Sassy sat on her bum a few feet away as she eyeballed him.

"Goddammit!" he exclaimed as he dropped his phone to the ground.

Hank hopped on one foot until he was able to lean against the cold, hard, marble coffee table. He glared at the dog. Sassy's stare was direct. She was sending a message. Hank's nostrils flared, and he gritted his teeth.

"Oh you wanna dance little doggie? Let's dance."

Hank charged at the pint-sized dog, no longer concerned about leaving a feces trail. As his hands descended downward to grab her, she gave a feisty bark and shot quickly between his legs around the corner, into the bedroom, and under the bed. Sassy stared at his pacing shoes from the darkness and safety under her mom's bed as he cursed and stomped his dirty shoe down again and again. He let out a guttural yell. Hank breathed heavily–his jaw locked. He stared at the bed. It was solid oak and heavy.

"That's ok, fucktard." Hank looked at the mess he had made on the floor. "I know what you care about. You won't win. I'm gonna win."

The pooch laid for a long time on her belly under the bed staring out at the open door where Hank had last been seen an hour earlier. He had stormed out the front door and slammed it behind him, but Sassy didn't trust him and worried it was a ruse to draw her out from her safe place. After a while, her speeding heart slowed, and she became more convinced of her safety, at least for the moment. Slowly, her eyes drooped and a deep sleep came over her.

Sassy heard a sweet humming. It was a familiar tune. Sassy tried to wake but found it difficult. Her eyes, try as she might, could only manage to crack, and through the small sliver, the dog could make out very little. Her eyesight was fuzzy, and it was too hard to keep them open. As they shut, Sassy thought they may never open again. The humming got louder. Was that Gilda? No, the sound was quiet yet distinctly masculine. Her nose itched. She could feel something was touching it, but her fatigue was winning. Sassy fought to open her eyes just enough to focus her hazy vision. There, just on the horizon of her snout, she could see a tiny flea with a top hat and a cane between her crossed eyes. Sassy was bewildered. Her normal instinct to crack it open with her teeth, dig and destroy, was absent. Sassy was in no condition for that. As the flea gave a twirl, it bowed its head and pulled the top hat off as it curtsied.

A polite flea, Sassy thought.

"Why so blue, friend?" The Flea asked as it straightened up. She lay there, motionless, as the gentleman flea removed his top hat with one of his skinny flea arms and rubbed his oily thorax with another. "Oh dear, trials and tribulations you shall have. That's in the good book you know, or so I'm told." He put his top hat on back on and gave it a pop on the top. "What you need, friend, is a pick me up! A little remembrance of time and space and all the woofs and bellows in between for all is not as it seems. Here, let me do my dance for you, and it will come back. It always comes back, right underneath the surface, friend."

Sassy's eyes flickered, fluttering from a spasms as the Flea danced along to the melody and light pulsated to the beat until everything disappeared and Sassy no longer worried about her eyes, or Hank, or anything else for that matter because she no longer seemed to exist, only the flea, only the dance, only...

Hours later, Sassy was awoken by yelling. Instinctively, she darted out from under the bed to defend Liza. She had just come in the front door, but before Sassy could rush to her, Hank slammed the bedroom door trapping the small dog inside. Despite her barks and howls, Sassy could do nothing as Hank berated and belittled her mommy. Liza cried.

Sassy twisted her head so that one eye could see under the crevice of the door. Liza was on her knees just a few feet away from the initial bowel movement. Hank had grabbed the back of her neck and had forced Liza's head down, putting her face inches from her dog's mess.

"Smell that? Do you smell that?" Hank's wrath was more than Sassy could bear. "Every time this dog does this, you're the one who's gonna pay, do you hear me Liza? You're gonna suffer, and you will feel it for days." Liza's head was shaking uncontrollably as she fought back against him to no avail. "The dog or me Liza. You have until tomorrow night to decide."

Sassy growled and barked. She scratched at the door. She howled in pain for her mom.

"Shut the fuck up!" Hank yelled at the door. He released Liza's neck from his grip. "We have an hour before the boys arrive, and you need to have shit ready. This place better be in tip-top shape when they get here, so I'd get to work, puddin'."

Sassy raised herself ready to pounce the moment the door opened.

Her voice shaking, Liza asked, "Can I go change?"

"No, you clean in your work clothes. And don't even think about taking off those heels. I'm really disappointed in you, Liza. Who gets a mutt like that? It's a lack of discipline. That's why that mutt is a fuck up. Structure, Liza. Dogs are like kids. They need structure and discipline."

The door never opened. Sassy's anger and rage slowly calmed. Blaring music could be heard coming from the stereo speakers in the other room. Sassy looked under the door and saw Liza scrubbing the carpet. After a while, Sassy retreated to sanctuary under the bed and dozed off again only to be awoken by loud voices sometime later coming from the other room. She ran from under the bed to the door and gave a bark. She peeked under the door but saw no one. Then she heard whimpering coming from atop the bed.

Hank paced along the perimeter of the dining table, lording over the other team members. Tommy was a young twenty-three-year-old with a t-shirt donning a likeness of Yoda that said "Church Of" over the picture. He pulled down on his sparse, teen-like goatee as he pondered.

"Come on, Tommy, this is a softball question. The female star who helped found United Artist was..." Hank asked grumpily. Tommy was nervous and his leg bounced up and down as he tugged on his facial fuzz, thinking.

"Why does he get the easy ones?" Asked Frank, a lanky man whose height was accentuated by his overly large pompadour. Frank played with the collar of his blue work shirt. He'd come over right after he'd added some Freon to the AC unit down the street.

"C'mon, Tommy!" Hank pointed at the Nakatomi Trophy with its miniature samurai sword. "We are never gonna win that trophy again at this rate!"

Tommy's leg shook faster.

Eric, an obese, partially balding man looked up from the pile of books he had open in front of him and wiped his forehead. "Kinda hot in here, Hank. Can we get the AC turned down?"

"Seriously?" Hank exclaimed. "We can't shift focus here. We can't worry about the fucking thermostat, Eric!"

Tommy's face lit up as the answer finally came to him. "Mary Pickford!"

"Yes, Tommy, about fucking time." Hank quickly acknowledged before turning his attention back to Eric.

"Seriously, man, any distractions could cost us. Turn the air down?"

Hank picked up the empty cookie container next to his teammate and shook it at him. "Try to say no to this shit, Eric. Maybe a little will power will keep us from having to use photoshop to get your fat ass in the team photo."

Eric shook his head and rolled his eyes. Hank didn't faze him. He smacked his lips and asked, "Do you have any more of those?"

The other guys laughed uncomfortably.

Hank tossed the bag at him. "Unfucking believable."

"I'm just askin'…" Eric used his forearm to wipe the last of the crumbs from his mouth.

Sassy Larue washed the mascara tinged tears from Liza's face with her little pink tongue as her mommy laid on the bed sideways cradling her. "I don't know what to do. I love you so much, but I need him."

Sassy licked with reckless abandon hoping every tear she lapped up would drive the pain away for Liza.

"Oh, my sweet Sassy. You know just what to do." She gave a small smile as she stroked the top of the dog's head. "Maybe he'll change his mind. Maybe tonight I'll do that thing he likes." She stopped, picturing the thing. "It's so gross." She walked herself through it in her dysfunctional mind. "But if it's my idea, he might change his mind."

The tears had stopped, and Sassy rubbed her head under Liza's chin.

"I wouldn't even know where to send you."

Sassy pressed her head harder into her chin.

"Alright, alright," Liza said as she stroked Sassy's backside. "I can fix this." Liza had a plan.

Hank opened the fridge and saw there was no more beer. "Fuck!" He yelled out. "Liza!" Hank's eyes wandered to Sassy's sweet milk. He called for her again. "Liza!"

"Yes?" she hollered from behind the closed bedroom door.

"We need more beer, now!" Hank snapped at her. Liza gave Sassy a kiss on her snout. "Gotta go, sweetums." She got off the bed, still wearing her work outfit. "On my way!" she announced as she straightened her outfit.

With a wry smile, Hank took out the milk and put it on the counter next to the sink. "A fitting last meal," he said to himself.

Later that night, as Sassy laid on the on the floor outside the closed bedroom door, she heard the muffled cries and other assorted noises that often accompanied the nightly ritual between Liza and Hank. Afterward, she heard quiet talking followed by sniffling and choked despair.

Sassy LaRue Descends Into Hell For A Bottle of Milk

Hank hummed as he moved lightly across the living room, swaying to a happy song. Sassy peeked at him while Liza readied herself for another day of work. Something was wrong. Sassy instinctively knew that. Liza would not make eye contact with her despite rubbing against her ankle, despite her calling to her with needy barks. Liza refused even the simplest of scratches or even a warm look. Liza wore bright pink with matching eye shadow. Sassy always thought it was such a good color for her. As Liza sat on the bed putting on her pink pumps, Sassy tried to entangle herself between her hands and the shoes, but Liza pushed her away roughly without any explanation. Sassy finally sat at her feet her with head cocked, confused.

As Liza kissed Hank goodbye, Sassy heard him whisper to her mommy. "Don't worry, I'll make today special for her." For a brief moment, Liza glanced at Sassy. Her bottom lip quivered as she turned away, and Hank closed the front door. "Have a good day, sunshine," he said. Hank stood with his back against the door, a broad smile on his face as he looked at the dog. Sassy was confused.

"Who wants some sweet milk?" He teased her. Sassy's ears perked up. "Oh, I know what sweet'ums wants."

Sassy cocked her head.

Hank slowly peeled himself from the door and moved toward the small kitchen. "Some sweet milk for the queen of the day? You want some sweet milk, flea bag?"

Sassy was bewildered. She'd never heard Hank use this tone of voice with her before. And she recognized the words her mommy always said to her. Sweet. Milk.

"Sweet milk for the dog from hell." Hank said kindly as he walked into the kitchen.

Sweet milk was enough to make Sassy's stump of a tail wag excitedly. Maybe Hank was turning a corner. Maybe the dirty thing Liza did had changed things? Sassy didn't trust the moment completely, but her love of that liquid treat was too much to bear, and she couldn't control the pitter patter of her own paws as she bounced her way towards her bowl in the kitchen.

Hank grabbed the milk off the counter and poured out its room temperature insides. The moment Hank cracked open the top of the container, the smell hit Sassy like a freight truck, and as the lumps of rotten milk splashed into her bowl, Sassy jumped back.

Hank laughed. "C'mon! Eat up, baby girl. It's full of protein, fucktard." Sassy growled at Hank as he mocked her.

That afternoon, Hank took Sassy for a walk. Much to her chagrin, they never made it to the sacred grass. Instead, Hank leaned up against a car in the parking lot and made himself comfortable mere feet from the grass he knew she longed for.

"Awww what's wrong? Don't want to go on the hot concrete, poor baby?" Hank needled her and then turned his attention to his phone.

Sassy heard the jangle of the bells again. Gilda was wearing her black workout pants and running shoes as she briskly made her way by the depressed pup and her tormentor. Sassy loved how Gilda always dressed up for a fast walk, her flowing multi colored blouse and dangling feather earrings swaying as she happily moved along.

As Gilda came upon them, she smiled at the pooch and said, "Good morning, Star child."

Sassy couldn't even muster a shake of her tail.

Hank looked up from his phone as she moved past. "You should say goodbye to her, you old witch".

Gilda without breaking stride nor turning her head replied, "You have no idea."

"Weirdo." Hank looked at the dog. "No one loves you. No one could ever love a beast like you." Hank tugged on Sassy's leash, and she looked up at him. "That's right, fucktard, look at me when I'm talking to you. I win. I always win."

Back in the apartment Hank began heating up some lunch while Sassy sat in the living room looking at an empty space on the wall where a picture used to hang of her and Liza. Hank put the overly loaded plate into the microwave and as it heated, he took out his cell and called Liza. He made sure it was on speaker phone. Sassy was lost in memories as she stared at the blank space on the wall. While the pup heard their voices talking she paid little attention until she heard her name.

"I found a place, a no kill shelter, I think she might be happy there." Liza said sadly.

"You know, babe, I've been thinking maybe we should give her to my little brother's kid, Sid." Hank announced.

"What?!" Liza exclaimed.

"Tone munchkin, tone." Hank scolded her, gently.

"Isn't that the kid who set his gerbil on fire?"

"Hey, that was like two years ago, and that was a one-off incident. He has a snake named Lee Harvey that's just fine. Had him like three years with no problems."

"Oh Hank, I just don't know."

"Babe, they live on two acres. It will be great."

"Hank I don't know."

"Good, it's done then. I'll call my brother."

"Hank," her voice desperate, "I'm just not sure."

Hank hung up.

The microwave beeped.

As Hank walked out of the kitchen, Sassy had not only left a pile for him but choreographed an intentional ass rub on the floor next to the message while staring intently into his eyes.

"Mother fucker!"

Hank threw his plate at the dog, and she moved nimbly out of the way and darted into the bedroom. She leapt with all her might onto the bed. Hank chased after but stopped cold as he entered the bedroom and saw Sassy standing atop his own pillow with her ass hovering an inch away from the pillow case.

"No, no, you little freak. Don't you dare." And with that, Sassy slammed her butt squarely on his pillow and rubbed her naked dog bottom about it furiously.

Hank dove onto the bed. His arm came down like a hammer just missing the dog as she nipped at his wrist, catching a fragment of skin. Hank's body lay sprawled across the bed on his stomach. He swung his arm spastically at the dog, and this time Sassy bit him on the forearm and broke his skin. He yelped and she jumped off the bed into the living room. Hank followed her around the corner, but Sassy caught him off guard and threw herself into his ankles. Hank, who was moving briskly, stumbled over the dog and fell hard. He found himself twisting in the air to right himself but wound up smashing the back of his head into the marble coffee table. The impact caused him to slam his jaws hard enough to make parts of his teeth crumble in his mouth and bite off the tip of his tongue.

Hank laid there, limp. His head bent awkwardly, upright it rested on one of the coffee table legs, his eyes half open. Blood seeped out of his crooked mouth. Sassy climbed up on his crotch and looked intently. Was he dead? Sassy noticed his chest rise and fall. Sassy wondered what to do next. Bite his throat? Push her body against his breathing holes?

Just then, the room began to get dark. Very dark. The sunshine that shone through the open blinds had gone black. Strangely, a spotlight appeared in the middle of Hank's chest. Sassy caught sight of a black dot flying into the spotlight. It was the top-hatted flea. Music began to play. The flea began to dance, swinging his cane lithely. As he moved gracefully in his shiny tap shoes, with a twirl he brought the cane down, tapping the tip and another flea popped up from that very spot. With another twirl and pop of the cane, another flea sprung up. The two new fleas didn't wear top hats like their creator, but they had choreographed dance moves and stepped in sync with the original flea. The leader stopped as his friends continued to sway and move.

"Hope you don't mind, Ms. Larue, but I brought a few friends." Sassy shifted her butt a bit, and her tongue hung out, amused. "I have quite a few friends, but have no worry, Ms. Larue, we mean you no harm." He called out, "Fellas!"

Suddenly, more fleas jumped into the spotlight. Four at a time, ten at a time, twenty. Before long, Hank's entire shallow breathing chest was black from an army of fleas who all danced in time simultaneously as the familiar song played. The dapper leader twirled in unison with his friends twisting, bending and leaping while he tapped his cane this way and that way. Sassy was mesmerized. Her stubby tail wagged in pleasure.

After several moves, the show crescendos with a horde of fleas jumping in and over each other as they spun and somersaulted into the air until finally, on the last note, they landed with their appendages out in what could be considered the largest insect jazz hand ensemble ever. Sassy barked with approval. They all bowed. Suddenly, a loud drum roll began, signaling the true finale.

The hatted flea raised his head and said, "And now, my friend, for our next number, we bring hell and all of its freedoms." The main flea turned towards Hank's face and his army did the same. He addressed Sassy formally, "Until next time, Ms. Larue."

The fancy flea leapt straight into Hank's left nostril. The drums continued and the crash of cymbals sounded as row after row of fleas jumped into Hank's nostrils. The aggressive beats got louder and louder as the fleas took over Hank's nose, and the skin expanded unnaturally. Sassy sat with her eyes wide. She watched his nose swell, and then she heard a snapping sound as his nose became crooked and broke. Finally, the last of the fleas entered and his nose was the size of a large orange. The drums continued and the fleas pulsating under his stretched skin. Hank began coughing, and his eyes shot open, wild and crazed. He immediately shot upward onto his feet, and Sassy was thrown to the side. The room was still dark, but Sassy could see his confused morbid movements.

Hank made guttural sounds as he spit blood and grabbed spastically at his oversized nose. The large, bulbous, knob blocked his vision. Hysterically, he dug his finger into his nose. Whatever the fleas were doing inside was painful, and Hank screamed. He couldn't get them out. Sassy sat back in wonderment but had to move as Hank swayed around the room uncontrollably.

Hank saw the dog and cried out, "Help me! Please, help me!" Sassy sat with her small but powerful tail dancing. "Oh God, someone help me!"

Hank frantically reached out in the dark and found the wall. Scattering his hands to-and-fro, he knocked pictures off the wall until he found the bookshelf, and his hands wrapped around the trophy. He brought it up towards his face, and the miniature samurai sword fell to the ground. He slammed the trophy into his face, over and over, extending his arms and then, with all his might, slamming the wood into his face as blood flew. Sassy scooted a bit to avoid a spurt without taking her gaze off the show.

Hank was nearly unconscious. His hands could no longer hold onto the trophy, and it fell to the ground as his arms went limp. He cried. His nose continued to gestate. Hank dropped to his knees. He screamed in pain again, and Hank's knuckles rested on the sword. With everything in him he gave a yell and grasped the blade. He forced himself to stab it upward into his assaulted nostrils. Blood exploded from his face holes with each jab, and his inhumane cries had no response of mercy. Sassy darted her tongue out touching her perfect nose. Her ears twitched every time his flesh popped from a newly created exit wound. Hank slowed his strokes, but he continued the attack on the invisible assailants in his nose even though there was barely any nose left to protect. The blade scraped his cheek bones. Most of his face gone. Finally, the microblade dropped, and Hank fell back.

Sassy climbed up on his chest. There was no sign of the fleas. Small breaths escaped from his face hole, and Sassy got up close to look deeply into Hank's empty eyes. A moment of recognition suddenly came over the lidless white orbs as a final gasp left. The room slowly filled with a natural atmosphere again. Sassy stared at the unrecognizable Hank. The front door opened. Sassy's tail danced and she jumped off his collapsed chest. The sound of the bells always made Sassy happy.

"Hello, sweet Ms. Larue." Gilda scooped the pooch up and gave her some scratches on her head. She looked at the corpse. "Fucktard." As she doted on Ms. Larue she said, "I think we need to find you a more responsible owner, and I have a friend who's just a bit of a celebrity. He will pamper you with all the care and love you deserve."

Sassy barked her approval and Gilda giggled.

Gilda turned and left the carcass that laid awkwardly on the floor. The two turned and walked out into the sunlight as Sassy's tail danced and Gilda hummed the chorus of "Puttin' on the Ritz."

J. P. Dildine

J.P. Dildine lives in Austin, Texas with his bad-ass wife and three pre-cocious, creative kids. Besides being weirdly addicted to drinks with umbrellas in them he sometimes writes. His first book "Toby Finkelstein and the Dandies of the Underworld" is will be out in early 2018 and he's currently running late on his appointment with life but is trying to remedy that.

shitishouldntsayblog.wordpress.com
www.facebook.com/jpdildine
twitter.com/JPDildine

Koalas

By Maxine Grey

"**M**um, are we nearly there yet?"

"Five minutes away, Cathy," responded Sheila, from the front of the car, glancing at her daughter briefly through the rear-view mirror.

"The car is just so hot, Mum! Why can't we just get a new car instead of driving everywhere in this hunk of junk all the time? The stupid air-conditioning doesn't work, and we live in Australia!"

Sheila gritted her teeth and bit back the retort she wanted to let fly at her eleven-year-old daughter. It was sweltering inside the old Holden Commodore she had owned for the last ten years, and despite the windows being down it made no difference–it was a roasting thirty-five degrees Celsius outside. Nothing but hot air blew in through the windows. Taking a deep breath, and counting to ten in her head, Sheila decided that she wasn't going to let anything ruin their day out together. After all, it was Cathy's eleventh birthday and she had been excited about this day out for weeks now.

Her daughter was an avid animal lover; if it moved and breathed, then Cathy adored it. She had asked to visit the Thompson's Creek Australian Wildlife Sanctuary months ago, and was particularly excited about having her photograph taken while cuddling a koala. Cathy was obsessed with koalas, she had books about them, pictures on her bedroom wall and a variety of stuffed versions sitting on her bed.

So here they were, in the sweltering Aussie heat, ready to meet and greet with some koalas.

Sheila wondered if the animals could shit or pee on people during the photography session. That would make her day really crappy and piss her off completely. She just hoped they were going to meet all the high expectations that Cathy had of them.

"There it is, Mum!" Cathy squealed with excitement, from the back seat of the old car. "I can see the big sign!"

Sheila turned on her left indicator and pulled the car into the wide driveway of the Wildlife Sanctuary, and followed the signs for visitor parking. After driving around for a few minutes, Sheila finally found a parking spot towards the back of the car park. She noted how many cars there were, and knew that the place was going to be heaving with people.

Bloody fantastic, she thought to herself. *That's all I need on a stinking hot summer's day, to be in close proximity to pulsing crowds of sweaty adults and noisy children.*

Slapping a fake smile on her face, Sheila took Cathy's hand and led her towards the front entrance of the park. It wasn't long before Cathy shook herself free of her mother's hand. Sheila sometimes forgot just how quickly Cathy was growing up. It reminded her to make the most of days like today. Sheila knew all too well from observing her close friends who had teenage children, that hanging around with their parents in public was not cool. It was only a matter of time before Cathy would be pulling away and asserting her independence more.

Ever since Cathy's dad had walked out their lives when Sheila was three months pregnant, she had vowed to raise her daughter to be close to her. She had been especially careful to be a real mum to Cathy, not a friend–a mistake she had seen happen with a few friends who were also single parents. Often fulfilling their personal needs for company and connection through their children.

It wasn't right, Sheila thought to herself. *Kids need to be kids, and I need to be a mum.*

It hadn't been easy raising Cathy on her own, but she wouldn't change it for the world. The bond they shared now was priceless, and Sheila took great comfort in knowing that Cathy trusted her immensely, and without question, to take care of her. A feeling that Sheila had not known in her own troubled childhood. Now, her beautiful daughter was eleven!

And beautiful … how beautiful she was.

Cathy was blessed with her father's golden blond hair, and the unique steely blue eyes that ran through the generations of Sheila's family. With straight teeth and beautiful pale skin with just a smattering of delicate freckles, Sheila knew that Cathy was going to be a hit with the boys once she was a bit older.

They will have to get through me first! Sheila thought to herself.

Only the very best will do for her girl. In contrast, Sheila's dark auburn hair and slightly olive complexion cast doubt, to some, on whether the two were actually related at all. If not for the similar eyes, no connection could be made.

Sheila paid the entry fee for the wildlife park, took the park map given to her by the customer service attendant, entered the facility, and spotted a shady rest area to stand and plan out their route with Cathy.

"Can we see the koalas before anything else, Mum? Please?"

Sheila wasn't a bit surprised at the request, knowing how eager her daughter was to see the cuddly icons of Australia.

"Come on! They are like real live teddy bears!" Cathy declared with excitement.

Sheila laughed at her daughter. "Okay, okay–let's go and see the koalas, or I'll never hear the end of it."

Checking the map and layout of the wildlife park, Sheila started walking towards the right-hand pathway. She was stunned at how many people were milling around. Being such a hot day in Sydney, Sheila had secretly hoped that families and tourists may have decided it was too warm to venture outdoors, but looking at the throngs of people, it wasn't to be. The place was packed.

At the start of the pathway was a man in a khaki uniform, selling cold drinks. Sheila bought two bottles of water, knowing how thirsty they were going to get in the hot sun. She had also made sure that herself and Cathy were well covered with sunscreen lotion before leaving the house earlier in the day. The last thing they needed was to go home and suffer in agony with a nasty sunburn. The sun bearing down on them was relentless. The Australian heat sometimes felt like it was suffocating, especially on days like today where there was not even the hint of a breeze to bring some much needed relief.

Sheila glanced around at the many tourists with their sun hats and caps on, their faces and bodies hidden behind sunglasses and dangling camera cases. They were easy to spot, the majority of them sauntered around with expensive cameras around their necks. Animals that are unique to Australia like the koala, the kangaroo, the wombat, the echidna and the dingoes were massive attractions for overseas visitors. The wildlife park allowed visitors to get up close and personal with many of the animals too; you could buy bags of feed for the kangaroos, and cuddle a koala whilst getting your photograph taken. It was this, in particular, that Cathy was so excited about. Something unique to treasure and remember her eleventh birthday.

They walked happily together, following the wooden signs that read "Koala Sanctuary". Neither of them had a care in the world. Life was good.

Gary, otherwise known as Gazza to the other koalas, was sitting in the highest gum tree in the Koala Sanctuary. His position as top dog, the alpha male amongst the others, had earned him the right to the tallest tree. A mighty fine gum tree it was indeed, covered with plenty of gum leaves and places to snooze. Gazza liked nothing more than a purge on gum leaves, followed by a nap.

Life is bloody beaut, he thought to himself, glancing down at his full, furry stomach.

He surveyed the horizon from his high position.

"Gazzaaaaa? Oi! Mate, you up there or what, cobber?" shouted Shaun, Gazza's best mate.

"Shit, yeah! Course I am. Does a bear shit in the woods or what?" responded Gazza

"Urm, not sure, Gazza, I've never talked to a bear and I know stupid people call us koala bears, but we're not related to bears at all. Anyway, we shit in the trees, gum trees, not the woods, eh?"

Gazza rolled his eyes and took a deep breath. A high IQ wasn't something that Shaun had been blessed with at birth. He was all brawn and no brain. Mind you, it was a known fact that all koalas had small brains, supposedly something to do with the boring limited diet of gum leaves. Shaun was a big, muscly hulk of a koala–mostly down to his regular morning workouts–chin-ups and sit-ups on the branches. Gazza was a bit jealous of Shaun, and it was common knowledge that Shaun could do three minutes, three whole fucking minutes of exercise before he fell into a koala nap! No other koala could last that long after exercising. Shaun was a bloody machine!

Gazza looked down to see Shaun heading up his way. It was usual for them to meet up this time of day to gasbag about the latest gossip in the camp, and share stories about their girlfriends. Sharon, better known as Shazza to the community, had been going out with Gazza for six months now. It was Gazza's longest relationship, mainly because Shazza could perform fucking miracles with gum leaves for breakfast, lunch and dinner. She was one hell of a cook. How Shaun pulled a girlfriend at all was beyond Gazza, but pull he did with Barbara, "Barbs" Wala. Shaun and Barbs had just started getting serious, and Shaun was now allowed to sleep on the same branch as Barbs.

She's an ugly one though, thought Gazza. *Face like she ran into the back of a truck. Maybe she did?* he pondered to himself. *Shit, didn't think of that, it might not be her fault.*

Not that koalas normally survived a hit by a truck. It was usually a lights-out scream and shout if that ever happened, on the busy roads that they stayed well clear of, protected within the sanctuary.

Shaun climbed up and sat opposite Gazza, hugging the ancient trunk of the big gum tree and promptly snapped off a gum leaf to chew on.

"What's up, Shaun?" said Gazza.

"Serious shit, that's what."

"No way?"

"Yes way, mate, yes fucking way!"

"Holy gum leaves, dude, what's wrong then?"

"Barbs has got that cleemeedeea disease, man!"

"You mean chlamydia?"

"Yeah, that's the one. Now, where is she gonna catch that from, eh?" Shaun spluttered, his voice tinged with anger.

"You don't think...?"

"I do, Gazza mate, 'fraid so—I think Barbs has been rooting around with some other fucker."

"Aww man, that sucks ... but she seems so in to you."

"Yeah, I thought so. She was complaining last week that I just sleep all the time and that when she is asleep, I'm awake and vice-versa, and that she is bored of it. Apparently we don't get enough quality time, whatever the heck that means," Shaun moaned.

Gazza scratched his hind leg, and looked at his best friend with concern.

"Well, that's not effing fair, mate! Does she not know that sleeping is one of the things koalas are famous for? We can't bloody help it, daft cow."

Shaun looked despondent. Gazza went to put a paw around his friend but quickly pulled it back to position it safely on the tree again, realizing his stupid stumpy arms were not going to reach, and that he was going to fall out of the bloody tree.

"There is a reason that koalas also get called *drop bears!*" Shaun spluttered.

"Mate, cheer up–maybe she just caught it from something else, eh?" Gazza encouraged.

"Yeah, maybe. I know she has it because I heard her talking to your girl Shazza about it. They were both complaining about how there's no sexual health drop-in center in the park. Apparently humans have got them every-where and they get that what's-it-called disease too".

"Chlamydia," Gazza reminded him.

"Yeah, that. Not that I know what it looks like or tastes like, mind you, she looks alright to me."

"Umm … it's … err, you know, down *there*."

"Down where? Bottom of the trees?"

"No, ya big dipstick! In her, um … furry bits."

"Furry bits? Which ones? Fur fucking everywhere, man."

"*Those* furry bits, you know–the secret chamber."

"Oh! right, gotcha mate–the man cave place. Don't know what it looks like myself, I've never been allowed in there."

"Jeez, Shaun, that's a bit much. I mean you are sharing sleeping branches!"

"Yeah, I know, and I eat her crappy gum leaf stew she makes all the bloody time."

Gazza gazed across the trees and saw that lots of the park's resident koalas were more active than usual. It was usually nap time at this period of the day. Well, it was nap time for most of the day really. They slept around eighteen hours a day and stuffed their faces with leaves when awake. Gazza was proud of the fact he could store huge amounts of munched up leaves in his cheek pouches. Sometimes, he would give Shazza a kiss and share it with her. True love that was.

He felt the fur stand up on his ears. Something just felt wrong, but he couldn't put his claw on it.

Shaun looked around with a sigh, wondered what Gazza was looking at, and scratched madly at a spot on his chest.

Bloody fleas! he thought to himself, before closing his eyes and drifting off into a deep sleep about gum leaf cheesecake and man caves.

"Look, Mum! Look up!" Cathy yelled excitedly.

"Oh yeah, how cute are they? Oh my God, how totally adorable are those koalas!"

"I know, right? Don't you just want to pinch one and take it home?"

"Over my dead body," Sheila whispered to herself.

"What did you say, Mum?" asked Cathy.

"Oh … um nothing, hun, just mumbling away to myself."

There were huge crowds gathered in the Koala Sanctuary–a huge wooden clock indicated that 11:00 a.m. was the next feeding time and opportunity to have photographs taken. It was 10:45; people were jammed in, side by side, like sardines on wooden bleachers, the seats designed to get a good view down onto a central area where two staff members stood patiently. They were easily identified by their khaki uniforms with the logo of the wildlife park on the shirt pocket.

"Quick, Mum, over here, I can see a good spot to sit." Cathy grabbed Sheila's hand and guided her to an empty spot between a young Asian couple and a noisy family with three children that they were trying – and failing – to keep under control.

"Excuse me," Sheila said to the couple as she sat down and tried to make room for Cathy. "Could you move along just a little bit, please?"

The young couple just looked at Sheila blankly and smiled, nodding their heads politely. Sheila realized that they may not understand much English, so she used her hands to indicate moving to the right a bit.

"Ah, yes, sorry, please, thank you," said the young man, who had obviously treated himself to a cork-hat. The corks swung from the brim of the hat, a design to keep pesky flies away, an iconic piece of fashion, one popular with tourists to Australia. She didn't have the heart to tell them that any self-respecting Australian wouldn't be seen dead in one. It was all good income for the Aussie economy, though. Australia had always been a popular holiday destination for tourists.

They can't cuddle a Koala anywhere else probably, Sheila thought to herself, smiling back at the young couple.

Shuffling along, the couple made room for Sheila and Cathy. It wasn't long before a voice boomed from a microphone announcing that the koala show was about to begin. Cathy squeezed Sheila's hand with excitement and bounced where she was sitting. Sheila smiled, feeling so much love for her daughter, and so glad she could make a wish come true today. It would be a day they would never forget, that's for sure.

The park attendant was telling the crowd a number of facts about the koalas; what they ate, their habitat, sleeping patterns and the fact that Koalas suffered a lot from chlamydia, a fact that surprised Sheila.

Poor buggers, she thought, *nasty STD that one. I wonder how they catch it?* She noted to Google more about it when she got home later.

Shaun awoke from his nap, not sure at first what had made him wake so suddenly.

"Ow, fuck!" he shouted, waking Gazza up with how loud he yelled. "Shit that hurts!"

"What's wrong, Shaun," asked Gazza.

"Dunno, but it feels like some really big bloody fleas are biting, and they really hurt!"

Gazza looked at his friend, who was scratching himself like mad, using his big strong claws to do it.

"Careful, Shaun, you'll do yourself an injury with your claws, man. Take it easy."

"Take it easy? I can't! I'm in agony ...*arrgh!*"

Shaun was really shouting and screaming now. It was freaking Gazza out; normally his best friend was cool, calm and collected but right now he resembled a manic mad koala.

Gazza could hear more shouting and screaming going on around him, from the other trees. He glanced over, and could see more koalas that he knew, and even those he didn't, scratching and itching the same way Shaun was. Suddenly, he spotted Barb and Shazza in a gum tree over to their left.

"Shazza! Hey, Shazza!" he yelled across the tree tops.

He could see that Barb was in a scratching frenzy also, and that Shazza was talking to her. She didn't seem to hear Gazza calling out to her.

"*Shazza!*" he shouted even louder. "*Are you okay?*"

Shazza looked over towards him, her pretty eyes turning towards in him in that super cute way that drove him nuts. He didn't think now was the time to ask for some branch-sharing, man cave rocking, however. Even Gazza had a sense of limits.

"Yeah, I'm fine, sweetie, but Barbs is in a bad way, she can't stop itching. She's clawing herself so hard I can see blood," she called over. "Is that Shaun with you*?*"

"Yeah, he's doing the same. What the fuck is going on?"

"I don't know," yelled Shazza. "Gazza, look around though…"

Gazza took in the horrific scenes all around him. Every single tree had a number of koalas in it; each and every one of them was going berserk with manic scratching, and the increasingly loud screaming was one of the most harrowing sounds he had ever heard. Something was really fucking wrong here. He briefly wondered if he should shimmy down the tree to get help, and then he remembered that humans didn't even know that they talked, so fat lot of good that was going to be.

They were fucked.

But wait, hang on.

How come he and Shazza were not scratching?

Before he had time to think too hard on the subject, Shaun suddenly let go of the tree trunk and Gazza watched him tumble down at a heck of a pace. At the same time, Cathy looked up into the trees and screamed at the top of her lungs as she watched the koala fall. Shaun hit the ground with a loud thump. The park visitors patiently waiting for the show all seemed to jump in unison, like someone had put a rocket up them. The park attendants, Nathan and Brad, stared at each other in horror before Nathan rushed towards the koala on the ground.

"Brad! Ring the park vet and get him down to the enclosure *now!*" yelled Nathan.

Nathan reached the koala and noticed blood matted through the fur, even his black button nose was scratched and bleeding. Nathan's first thought was that the poor thing hurt itself crashing into the branches on the trip down the tall gum tree, but then the injured koala raised its right paw slowly and starting to scratch itself, leaving deep gashes on its stomach. A strange keening noise was coming from the koala; Nathan was shocked it was even still alive. It had fallen from such a height.

"Tell the vet it's alive! *But hurry!*" screeched Nathan to Brad, who was on the mobile phone to the vet center at the top of the park. "Nobody taught me mouth to mouth or CPR for a fucking koala when I took this job!"

Nathan watched in horror as the poor animal writhed in agony and rocked back and forth, now scratching itself with both paws; those long, huge claws were doing some serious damage. He reached out and tried to grab hold of the koala's paws, and got scratched badly across both hands for his effort.

"Argh! *Jesus Christ that hurt,*" he screamed.

Brad was now off the phone and speaking via microphone to the crowd that were on their feet, watching Nathan near the fallen koala in horror.

"Please, sit down ladies and gentlemen, there is nothing to worry about, the vet is on his way, but I need you to please just sit down and stay calm and remain within the enclosure for now. Thank you for your cooperation". He could sense the panic in the air.

Cathy looked at her mum in horror, and then started to push people out of the way, climbing over legs and feet, heading towards the koala on the ground and the keeper standing over it.

"*Cathy! Stop!*" shouted Sheila, as she helplessly watched Cathy's head bob through the crowd of people.

She knew it was futile, he daughter was on a mission and she wasn't going to just stand by and be a spectator. She was a strong-willed girl and once she set her mind to something, that was it. Sheila had no choice but to run after Cathy, fearful of losing her in the heaving throng of people, all of whom carried an aura of panic about them now.

Asking them to stay calm was a bit of a tall order, Sheila thought, as she pushed people out of her way, her gaze following Cathy's blonde hair up ahead, like a beacon.

On the ground, the koala started to spasm and jerk like he was being electrocuted. His arms and legs were shaking and he was now banging his head off the ground. The eerie scream coming from his tiny mouth was unearthly and loud. It echoed in the tall trees.

Brad's training instincts kicked into action. He stepped past Nathan, and put his hand underneath the furry head in a futile effort to stop any further damage from the repetitive head banging off the ground. As he leaned over and got one hand under the koalas head, he found he was leaning right over, almost nose to nose. He found himself intimately face to face with this lovely animal and felt a desperation to save it, no matter what.

He looked at the pitiful, struggling koala.

The beady black eyes were closed.

Before Brad knew what was happening, he felt a sharp agonizing pain on both sides of his neck. It felt like someone was trying to tear his head off.

Blood was spurting in an arc and Brad could see it spattering the gum trees and leaves behind the koala. For a second, he briefly wondered who's blood it was. Looking down through the agony, he locked eyes with the tiny koala and as more blood pumped out of his cut jugular vein, he saw nothing but pure evil, evil where there should be cute button eyes. Instead, he saw dark black pools and felt like his very soul had been taken.

It didn't take long for Brad to bleed out and fall to the side of the koala, one of his arms casually flung over the koala's torso as though giving him a hug. There was blood everywhere, including all over the fallen koala, the ground, the leaves, and the tree bark. Human blood was spilt for the first time in the Koala Sanctuary.

Cathy had been almost to the spot where Brad was trying to help the koala when she saw the koala lift up both of its short arms and seem to pull Brad down towards its face, as though to engage in a kiss. She watched in horror as the giant lethal claws dug into the sides of Brad's neck and ripped out skin, muscle and tissue. Cathy could see exposed bone on the left side of Brad's neck. Frozen to the spot, Cathy could only watch on helplessly as fear turned her stomach inside out, and she felt the warm trickle of urine running down her legs. She whimpered, trying to find her voice to scream, but couldn't.

The gawping crowd had witnessed everything, and as news reports would later attest, the sound of screaming could be heard for miles around. People stood up and started to clamber over seats and each other in a bid to get out of the area, total panic was in the air and it was every man and woman for themselves. A number of people fell and were trampled underfoot in the crush to climb up over the seats back to the main footpath. The Asian tourist in the cork-hat lay helplessly as heavy feet thundered down on his chest, crushing his ribs whilst his wife tried frantically to pull him up by his arms. It was useless, the crowd of people had all the momentum of a human tsunami.

Cathy looked desperately for her mum, but could not see her in the chaos that was the swarm of bodies before her eyes. She really wanted her mum, more than ever before. As Cathy stood there, her eyes widened in stunned shock as more and more koalas started to drop from the gum trees, falling down into the koala sanctuary arena and landing on the floor beneath the trees. Every single one of them was scratching at its body and creating huge bloody gashes without seeming to notice or feel any pain. The full body spasms came next, and Cathy looked up just in time to see Nathan, the other keeper, run towards her and grab her hand telling her to run.

Adrenaline pulsing through her veins, Cathy's legs were pumping like pistons, her years of winning races at school suddenly coming back to her. She felt the sweaty hand of Nathan in her own and realized she was keeping up with his frantic pace. Suddenly, Nathan stumbled, let go of her hand and crashed to the ground, face first.

"Get up! *Get up!*" Cathy screamed at him.

Grabbing his left arm, Cathy started tugging at him, wishing him to regain his footing. The sense of urgency she felt was terrifying her, and the thought of running on alone was just too much. Nathan was not moving at all, and Cathy saw that he had a large cut on his forehead. It was bleeding profusely and Cathy could see that Nathan had hit his head on a very large rock.

I'm on my own now, she thought.

"No, no, no, no!" Cathy cried, feeling unbridled terror course through her whole being.

Torn between staying with him, getting help and finding her mum, Cathy decided that she needed her mum more than anything else. Mums always know what to do, right? With a last look at Nathan lying prone on the ground, Cathy turned around and started running back towards the Koala Sanctuary enclosure. She could feel her heart nearly beating out of her chest and her lungs hurt so much from the exertion.

Sheila had been bustled up with the panicking, surging crowd after the koalas all came down to the ground, and her efforts to push against the flow and try to get to Cathy were useless. It was either go in the other direction, or stay and be crushed to death in the throng of bodies. She managed to reach the top of the tiered seating area and stood on the pavement alongside many others. Out of breath, and terrified for Cathy, Sheila looked down at the spot where they were both sitting only ten minutes earlier and tried to compute what her eyes were seeing.

There were at least thirty koalas, many with shreds of bloody fur and skin hanging off them from their own self-inflicted crazed scratching. Each had eyes that were pitch black, glistening like onyx. In amazement, Sheila watched them start to climb over the wooden seats and rapidly advance towards the crowd of onlookers. Those that had stayed to look back didn't take long to kick into gear and start running again, the collective screams deafening as they went. Sheila couldn't believe what she was seeing, but she wasn't keen to stay to find out what was coming next so started to run, her legs seeming like lead as she pushed one foot out in front of the other. This wasn't happening, it just *couldn't* be happening. These were the cute little koalas, the "bears" that the world loved so much! A national symbol of Australia and all things good. This was going to no doubt kick a big hole in the Australian Tourism dollar.

The koalas looked like rabid dogs, frothing at the mouth and dripping foam as they too ran after the throngs of terrified visitors, preying on the helpless. They seemed to have obtained supernatural speed and strength and were moving in small packs with a single focus on the people in front of them. They were gaining ground, and the gap was narrowing between man and nature.

Sheila had managed to get ahead of the bulk of the crowd; most were heading for the front gates and trying to get out, but some had split off on separate paths in panic and desperation, looking for somewhere to hide. It turned out that this was a really bad idea. Looking like superhero demonic teddy bears, a pack of koalas bore down on a group of people heading towards a toilet block for refuge.

They launched themselves on the terrified people, ripping and tearing at any part of the body they could latch on to, their huge black claws like slicing talons. There was no mercy as people were quickly gutted, their steaming intestines spilling out on the pavement like tubular spaghetti. Others lost their eyes as their faces were literally clawed away and ripped to shreds. The screaming was deafening. It was a total blood bath, and the koalas seemed to be gaining more strength and a bigger desire to kill.

They wouldn't stop until everyone was dead.

They had briefly sated the burning hunger inside them but it wasn't enough. The pack ran back up the path to join more of their kin heading towards the main entrance, and the bulk of the people left alive.

Cathy got back to the koala area, and witnessed the throng of koalas heading over the last row of chairs. She could hear the terrified screams of people in the near distance, and a deep fear took hold as she pictured her mum being gouged and ripped open by one or more of the creatures she loved so much. Cathy began to cry; great, gulping sobs that racked her entire frame. The hot tears spilled down her face and she sat down on the ground before her legs buckled and gave way on her.

My life is over, it's never going to be the same again and it's all my fault, she thought to herself angrily.

If she had never asked to come to the park and see the koalas, her mum would be with her right now, on her special day. She had messed everything up.

Shazza and Gazza had witnessed the horror that had unfolded. First, Shaun had gone berserk, and his fellow koalas had followed suit. Clinging to each other, they were sitting in a gum tree while looking down on Cathy, and listening to the distant screams of people dying at the hands of their friends. *Their friends!*

"Shazza, we need to do something," whispered Gazza, as he looked at Cathy's sobbing body on the ground.

"Sure, Gazza, any bright ideas? Throw ourselves in the middle of our frenzied mates who have all totally lost the plot and been possessed by the devil?" Shazza responded, looking at him in fear.

"Come on, let's go down to that girl, maybe we can help her. I know it's the rule never ever to talk to humans, but at a time like this I think we can really throw the rulebook out the bloody window, love."

"Gazza, you had better know what you are doing or we are over, do you hear me?" Shazza spat at him, knowing she was really speaking from a place of fear.

Slowly, they moved down the trees, moving down between the branches until they reached the floor of the enclosure. Moving quietly, together, they approached Cathy from behind. Cathy was sobbing loudly and unable to hear the approach of the two koalas. Gazza tapped her gently on the shoulder.

"Aargh!" Cathy screamed, peddling backwards on the ground, scrambling to get away.

"It's okay, we're not here to hurt you. We want to try and help."

"You are … are talking? What? Koalas don't *talk!*" Cathy stuttered, and decided she was both hallucinating through her eyes and ears.

"Well, actually we do, sweetie," said Shazza gently, inching forward towards Cathy. "It's just we don't let humans know that, as that would be the end of our peaceful existence, you see? Mind you, it seems koala Armageddon came early today!"

"Wow! I can't believe I'm hearing this!" Cathy exclaimed, forgetting for a moment the situation she was in. "Wait until I tell my mum!"

Silence fell on the three of them as they all looked at each other with sad eyes.

"Is my mum dead?" Cathy whispered. "Did the koalas hurt her?"

"We don't know, but we are sure as hell going to find out, love." Gazza spoke as he extended his paw to Cathy in an invitation to come with them.

Cathy had to trust them, right? She had to trust they were not like the other koalas. She knew she had to be brave, it was the only way she might be able to find her mum. She reckoned her mum was probably dead by now, but a small part of her held on to some hope that she would find her alive.

Cathy, Gazza and Shazza all climbed the seat tiers to the top of the pathway and started running towards the sounds of screaming and crying near the front of the wildlife park.

2 DAYS LATER

Cathy sat at the kitchen table, pushing the chops and peas around her plate. She wasn't hungry, the food made her feel sick. She felt sick all the time, now.

"Come on, love, try and eat a little bit for Grandma, huh?"

Cathy looked up at her grandma and noticed how steely blue her eyes were; so much like her own, and they were set in the wrinkles around her eyes that her grandpa called laugh crinkles. She knew her grandma was trying to help, but she was tired of trying to tell them about what had happened with Shazza and Gazza back at the wildlife park. They didn't believe her that two of the only seemingly normal koalas at the sanctuary talked to her, and led her right to her mum. The police didn't believe her, either. Nobody believed her. She was told she had a vivid imagination, and had heard whispers that she was saying it as "a coping strategy," whatever one of those was.

But they *had* talked, and they had helped her find her mum. In her heart, she was so grateful to them for that, and just wanted everyone to know how special they are.

The theme tune to the Six O' Clock news came on and Cathy turned to the TV. They were still reporting on the massacre at the wildlife park. In total, sixty-four visitors were found massacred and dead, twenty-one were seriously injured and only seven escaped with their lives. Once the staff at the park saw what was happening, they had attempted to subdue the crazed koalas with tranquilizer guns, managing to bring a number of them down, but some had already escaped over the metal barrier gate and were eventually killed by police on a hunt that lasted for twenty-four hours. It was believed that no koala was left alive.

Cathy knew different. She had watched Shazza and Gazza leave the park by escaping through a small hole in the fence near the front entrance. They had turned to wave goodbye and her heart had burst into a million pieces. She desperately wanted to see them again. They were gone, hopefully to a safe place.

She had found her mum, or what was left of her. The body was strewn on a grassy area near the customer service kiosk and her mother's head was almost torn completely off, such force had been used that was unimaginable in such a small animal. It was obvious that her mother had put up a fight as her hands were in shreds from the claws of whatever koala or koalas had taken her down. Huge gashes in her wrists and arms proved this too. Cathy had sat with the body until the police arrived with body bags and stretchers to take her mum away.

Cathy was living with her grandparents now, her mother's parents, and she missed her mum terribly. She caught the last bit of the news report where scientists who had done autopsies on the bodies of dead koalas had announced that the change in nature and aggressive killing streak seemed to stem from an unknown breed of flea that the koalas were infested with.

They were working on an antidote for this flea to administer to all koalas around Australia.

Cathy didn't hate koalas. How could she? Two had helped her, and kept her alive. She knew the whole world feared them and many despised them now, though. It made her angry because, for centuries, humans had been killing off animals through their own greed, ignorance and sheer inhumane capabilities. Nature turned. No doubt it would turn again somewhere, sometime.

A government warning was issued stating that no person could any longer have their photo taken cuddling a koala, just in case.

4 DAYS LATER

The hot, unyielding Australian sun was beating down on the kangaroo enclosure at Sydney's Taronga Zoo. The temperature was soaring over forty degrees Celsius, and the shaded areas were filled with kangaroos as they lazed in the cool dust. Crowds of fascinated tourists and zoo visitors were watching through the windows. Children pointed and shouted in their excitement at viewing one of Australia's hallmark animals.

"Steve, I feel really fucking itchy, mate," blurted Dave, one of the Kangaroos.

"What type of itchy? Like the shitty fleas that we are riddled with?" Steve threw back lazily, scratching his own tail with his long front legs and claws.

"Nah mate, this is like *really* fucking itchy."

Maxine Grey

Maxine Grey is the pen name of Maxine Groves. Born in the UK and after 30 years spent living in Australia she is now residing back in the North East of England.

She writes horror, dark psychological fiction and crime and is also a reader, reviewer and Book Publicist. Maxine only put pen to paper to start writing in 2017, remembering the words of her English High School Teacher that one day she would write a book.

Later in 2017 you will see more of Maxine's stories in various horror anthologies. Maxine is working on a crime/horror novella due for publication early in 2018 and also her first novel, a psychological thriller/ crime blend.

Maxine reads a book a day on average and can't live without her books. She is also the owner of 2 very naughty Burmese cats who are constantly interrupting the creative process, usually wanting snacks.

www.facebook.com/maxinegreybooks

www.twitter.com/maxinegreybooks

Aww Nuts!

By L. E. Perez

Those damned bloody memes. They were everywhere. Squirrels dancing, squirrels eating, squirrels unzipping their fur to show their super colors. It was ridiculous. No self-respecting squirrel would let themselves be photographed, but Ser Quirrel was different. He loved posing and wreaking havoc where he could. It had gotten to the point that squirrels were the one animal no one took seriously and that is exactly what he had been working toward.

Ser Quirrel loved his life. I mean really, how many people got to be reincarnated into their favorite animal.

As a human, he'd been a merchant, a boring merchant who longed for a life of adventure. He dreamed of sailing the seas instead of shipping goods for the Spanish government. But God had another plan for him and a merchant he was, until the dark priest had shown up on the docks with a proposal.

You see, as a child he'd been left for dead on the docks by his mother. She had made a deal however, her son's life for her wealth. His life had never belonged to him at all. The dreams he had, the wants, they belonged to the dark priest.

The night the priest showed up he made Quirrel a deal. Choose an animal to live as or he would take his life as promised by his mother. When he'd asked why, the priest had told him animals were the key to eternal life but a human life would be forfeit. With no real options, Quirrel accepted and he was reborn as a squirrel.

The dark priest had attempted to capture him but Quirrel was having none of it and he had escaped. That had been over five hundred years ago.

Looking over his kingdom, or as it was otherwise known as, Central Park, he giggled. Everyone else heard a chirp which was always oh so cute. But he wasn't cute. Over five hundred years he'd been attacked, almost eaten and drowned trying to get across the ocean but he realized something. The dark priest had given him eternal life as long as he didn't find him. But he'd come close. In the last hundred years the priest had tracked him down to the East Coast but he hadn't been able to find him in the park.

That's where the memes came in. Ser Quirrel was able to do things no other squirrel could and the other squirrels knew it. They followed him and responded to his demands and commands. They were cute, they were funny and they were loved. Then came the rains.

The dark priest had managed to make it rain along the east coast for over five days and the flooding in the park had forced some of his furry friends and him out into the public. The priest had caught a glimpse of him and had him cornered in the park now. He didn't want to stop living. Granted he wasn't human anymore but he still enjoyed life and the pleasures of life, so he had a plan. If he could expose the priest maybe he would be able to get his little friends to stop being cute and be what they really were. Vicious little rodents in a cute furry package. The memes were his fault. He sent them out to do stuff all the time and people were always taking pictures.

He giggled again wondering if the people would take pictures of the priest as he was taken down by squirrels. No matter, now that the rains had ended, it was time. Quirrel called his friends together by the entrance near the museum. They didn't comprehend as he did but they got the gist and little fangs made their appearance as their true natures were revealed. He sent a few out to find the priest and draw him to them. He didn't have to wait long.

The priest hid in plain view, as did he. He was dressed in a tan suit and carried the same satchel Quirrel remembered from the docks oh so long ago. Unfortunately, he didn't come alone.

The group of children spread out across the playground while he took a seat on one of the park benches and smiled.

Quirrel hesitated.He didn't want to do this in front of children but this was his life. He closed his eyes and concentrated. He had learned over five hundred years how to control the like animals around him and as he pictured the priest in his mind, all the squirrels in the area turned to face him.

The squirrels started chirping, squeaking, mewling, the sound was deafening and the children stopped what they were doing as the sound drowned them out.

"Mr Quirrel, what's going on?" The little boy who asked the question looked at the man in the tan suit and back toward the squirrels that started to gather.

Ser Quirrel stopped. Quirrel? How could *his* name be Quirrel. His name was Quirrel!

He stepped out into the open and looked at the priest. It was him. The person in the tan suit looked like him five hundred years ago before he was a squirrel. He didn't understand until Mr Quirrel started laughing.

It clicked. Animals were the key to eternal life. That's what the dark priest had said and then he'd woken as a squirrel. The priest had taken his life, his body and put him into a squirrel. A squirrel! Anger raged in him. His chirping grew louder, his screeching made the dark priest place his hands over his ears.

That's when they attacked. Squirrels swarmed across the park toward Mr Quirrel and the children even as he started keening. His keening guided the squirrels toward their target and the dark priest ran. He left the children behind him to be bitten and buried by the mass of squirrels descending on the very location Mr Quirrel once stood.

He placed a thought in their cute furry little heads. *Bring him to me.*

It took only a few minutes and he followed the squirrels as they dragged the new Mr Quirrel over to the lake. He was bleeding and cut from being dragged.

Ser Quirrel looked down at the man who had taken his place. Eternal life. He didn't know if he should be happy or angry, the feelings warred in him but he didn't know why.

He couldn't speak so he chirped and chirped. Squeaked and keened and the man he knew as the dark priest, who now wore his face, just laughed.

"You wonder why you've been blessed or cursed by this life."

Ser Quirrel chirped angrily and ran up to him coming up on his haunches. They were eye to eye now and there was no sign of the cute squirrel from the memes people knew. This was a vicious rodent.

"You were destined from birth to live this life."

Ser Quirrel let out a screech and bit him on the nose. Mr Quirrel shook him off and tried to bring up his hands but Ser Quirrel bit those too.

"Stop!" The dark priest's voice changed and he breathed into the face of the squirrel he had damned allowing him to once again use his human voice. "Speak."

Ser Quirrel tried to say something but only a squeak came out. He concentrated as hard as he could and spit out the words he'd been wanting to say for over five hundred years. "Why?" He squeaked.

The dark priest stood up, brushing off the squirrels who held him and laughed. "You really don't know? You're Spanish, your name. You've always been a squirrel!"

Ser Quirrel had zero regrets when he allowed his friends to swarm the dark priest. He got the joke now, but the joke was on the priest. If he couldn't live in his own body, no one would.

Screams echoed through the park as night fell and Ser Quirrel giggled again. Ser Quirrel, To be a squirrel, he got, but it really wasn't funny.

L. E. Perez

Born and raised in New York City, L.E. moved to Scranton to raise her children. Once they were teenagers, they moved to Northern Virginia. Now? She enjoys the warmth in Orlando with her honey.

A lot like her first character Leigh, she's worked in corrections, probation, and victim services (not police)...She's done a little of everything. She is a 4th degree Black Belt and believes in believable fight scenes.

She believes in her mantra: STRONG WOMEN, STRONG STORIES.

She writes the stories that need to be written. She currently has stories in a variety of genres. Romance, Thriller, Urban Fantasy, Paranormal Romance, and more...

Stay tuned for more!

www.leperez.com
www.amazon.com/L.E.-Perez/e/B00ASREREU
www.facebook.com/LEPerezNovelreads
www.instagram.com/leperezauthor
www.twitter.com/Honorcpt

THE CHAOS CONTINUES...
DEMONIC ANTHOLOGY COLLECTION

Demonic Wildlife
Demonic Household
Demonic Carnival
Demonic Classics
Demonic Vacations
Demonic Medicine
Demonic Workplace
& more to follow!

More books from 4 Horsemen Publications

Crime, Detective, and Noir

Joe Davison
Journey to Hell

Mark Atley
Too Late to Say Goodbye
Trouble Weighs a Ton

Horror, Thriller, & Suspense

Alan Berkshire
Jungle

Amanda Byrd
Trapped

Erika Lance
Jimmy
Illusions of Happiness
No Place for Happiness
I Hunt You

Maria DeVivo
Witch of the Black Circle
Witch of the Red Thorn

Mark Tarrant
The Death Riders
Howl of the Windigo
Guts and Garter Belts

Discover more at 4HorsemenPublications.com